MISERY'S COMPANY

MISERY'S COMPANY

Leslie Wootton

MISERY'S COMPANY

iUniverse books may be ordered through booksellers or by contacting:

iUniverse
1663 Liberty Drive
Bloomington, IN 47403
www.iuniverse.com
1-800-Authors (1-800-288-4677)

ISBN: 978-1-5320-7825-5 (sc)
ISBN: 978-1-5320-7826-2 (e)

Library of Congress Control Number: 2019909842

Print information available on the last page.

iUniverse rev. date: 07/31/2019

PROLOGUE

They killed her.

Whatever it took, they killed her.

Standing alone in an unfamiliar room, Robert Garin Carlyle was terrified to be alive. His dazed state of mind didn't help things one bit. He didn't know if he was going to be sick, or if he was thirsty, or what. He struggled to remember how he got where he was and felt pathetic about it. Yet again he failed to master even his own thoughts. He looked aimlessly around the room desperately searching for someone who was not there. The room was in a state of disorganization, but it was nothing compared to the chaos within his head. He would not be capable of reciting his own name if someone requested it of him. Fortunately for him there was no one else around. She was not there. She was still back where he left her, but not as he wished her to be. He was so scared he trembled.

Yet she still called to him. She owned his will. She owned his state of mind. She was drawing him to her even though he had run away to get back to here.

She.

She was no longer there. At least not as he wished she was. She was not as anyone wished to be... except those who did show up. He couldn't remember clearly. He struggled to remember details, and the cloudiness thickened. They were there because she was there. Now he is gone because she is gone. Well, her body is still there. They left it there.

He left it there. Her. He left *her* there.

He was a coward. He wished he had never been there to begin with. More importantly, he wished she never had been there. Her body was still there. Still there now.

Why were they there anyways? He could not figure it out. He knew they were there for her. They got their wish, but why? Why did they want her? Why did they come after her?

He wondered if he should return. Or, perhaps, if he never should have run away. It was all he knew to do: run. A cataclysm of thought perplexed him. His mind went blank, he could not think. Or was his mind overfilled with thought? He did not know. He did not have the strength.

Panic. Absolute panic.

He looked around the room to try and focus. Nothing looked familiar to him. Searching for something to fix his mind onto and settle down, he found a mirror. The man looking back at him was not who he wanted to see. It never was. He never had amounted to the man he wished he really was.

He saw his hair and remembered the haircut he had before he came out to see her. He had asked the stylist to cut it like the picture he'd brought in. It wasn't even a celebrity. It was a clipping from an insurance ad. He thought the man looked "normal" which is what he wanted to be. But with his dark hair cut this short, it only drew attention to how overweight he was. That his loose clothes didn't fit and that his cheeks were chubby.

Then in the mirror he saw behind him. He could see couch and the clothes pile that was not his. The color of the walls and the multitoned carpet. He had seen all these things in a picture. Not a picture she'd sent him, just one he found on her social media.

These are all her things, this is her room. *Was* her room. Not her things any longer. Or were they? He didn't know. He hated getting caught up in the monotony of thought. So many thoughts. Only she was normally all of his thoughts. And now her room. And this stuff.

He didn't know what he needed or if he should stay. He had to go… but was that running? Running away? He tried hard to think if he knew enough to go to the police. He struggled to understand if it would be more of a report or a confession. The chaos in his mind still consumed him. Filled his mind. He couldn't make a decision at all. He was never good at that, only now he had a decent excuse instead of his usual.

As though it were his mind overflowing, he vomited. He did not even have warning, it just happened. Like coffee over the lip of a cup as more coffee kept being poured in, his mind could not properly relieve the pressure. He was still confused and still filled with thoughts. Cloudy, chaotic, unorganized thoughts he could not comprehend.

And it would not stop.

"There were so many of them." He said aloud before his memory could really grasp the concept. But how many were there? He closed his eyes in painful memory. Trying to recall the details, but desperately trying to forget. "They wouldn't stop. They just kept going." He shook his head as more questions came to mind faster than words could leave his mouth. He put his head into his hands and cried. There was no one to console him, no one to answer his questions… except himself. But that would require him to remember.

He looked up in thought working his mind through the process. He had walked away, no, run. Run away from the park and past a café. No, he *walked* past the café. He looked down at his hands like a fortune teller trying to find insight to the future. His past he could not see clearly, but he knew he had fled in terror. He was no hero. Especially now looking at his hands and coming to the realization they were not clean. He grimaced as he realized what covered his hands, arms and clothes.

Blood.

"Is it even today?" He shook his head and wiped his hands on his pants. Opening his eyes, he began to regroup, "Of course it's today, and this happened today. It's not over." Tears began to fall again as his mind filled to the top. Again, he looked at his hands for clarity.

The dirt and blood on his hands was a clearer vision than anything his memory was searching for.

"I have no cuts. Why not? Even if they didn't cut me I should have cut myself in that fury. I may have. It's likely. How could I know? I could look." He wiped his hands together in search of a wound. Desperate now to see if this was his blood or someone else's. Or hers. How would he know? With pain again, he closed his eyes and made a grip like he was holding a knife.

"When did I get the knife? Was it a knife? Lords! Remind me!"

Panicked, he looked around and immediately took it back, saying, "I do not want to know. I feel sick." His hands down on his knees, vomit again, only now not so much.

He opened his weak hand as though the memory of him holding a knife suddenly vanished, "He pulled a knife. That's self-defense. Right?" Without any injuries he could find, he doubted self-defense would hold up. They never attacked him, just her. They only went after her even with him right by her side. He was right there the whole time.

His hand came to form a grip again, and with feigned strength he stated, "I did have a knife." Falling to his knees he released the imaginary knife onto the carpet in the front room. The battle in his head was as great as the battle he could barely remember. He lay down praying for sleep to defeat him and take away his memory. Whether it was to be closer to her, or to remove the thought of her completely, exhaustion finally overtook reality.

WAVERTREE

The Park where it all begins. Quirky. Simple.
A place of beginnings.

(I)

Even with this morning's daze I am thinking more clearly. The aftermath of a mad fury can be so unclear. Like I would know. I do not really remember being actually mad, more like scared than anything. I remember better now; the knife was never intended for me. Never pointed my way. Her way. I may never know why. She had nothing.

She had everything I ever wanted.

There could never be another woman like her. I'm done. She's gone. I'm gone. This is not to be a love chronicle. End that.

How many? Four of them? Five? Pretty sure it was five. No, couldn't be. I can only distinctly remember two. Did one of them get away? They had no interest in fleeing. No more than three. I think. They didn't scream or cry. I certainly did. Should they have? They just wanted her dead. If they would have attacked all at once I couldn't have succeeded in what I did. One or two of them maybe. That was too easy. Exhausting. But I should not have succeeded in that battle.

That's why. That's right. They were after her. Not me.
They chose poorly. What did she have? Nothing.

Everything.

I will be forever plagued.
What did she have? What did they have?
I should have searched them. Maybe. I still can.
I am safe for the moment, at least. Whatever safe is. It was dark when I got here, I cannot imagine anyone saw me. Not that late at night. What time is it now? How long did I sleep? It's still dark out, but is it the same day? I need to get my things together. My things? Or just what I need now?

Her things are everywhere. My things are just for travel. Books. Language CDs. Notepads and pens. Maps of cities unknown to me. I must gather things for speed. I don't see my backpack. I find a sports bag of hers and move my sturdiest clothes to it.

Did I only bring dress shoes and one shitty pair of old sneakers?

In a drawer next to her bedside I find it is empty except for 3 cigarettes in a pack and a leather-bound diary. I take a cigarette and walk the house looking for a light. The stove will have to do. My mind is calming. I actually pause to wonder how she would feel about me smoking in her home. Back in her room I take the two remaining cigarettes and tuck them into the diary's binding.

I fumble with the awkwardness of a cigarette in my hand and cough as I take a drag. I convince myself that this will be soothing. I look pathetic, I'm sure of it.

Her diary is the only thing I take with me that is not fit for survival away from the comfort of a city that I know. Perhaps her words will be enough for survival alone.

Will it be enough? What did she have to say? Are there clues?

Or just more madness awaiting me? Why do I suddenly see the city as a wilderness I must hide within? Am I truly being chased? Are they hunting me?

The cigarette leaves me dizzy. I suddenly feel the same way I felt last night. Again, I vomit, but only can dry heave. I see the arm of the couch where I must have been facing last night. Somehow the sight of my own dried vomit settles my stomach. I put the cigarette out half burned and try to flip the butt into the kitchen, assuming it will fall perfectly into the sink. I miss, and it doesn't even leave my hand, it just breaks. Even though I put the ember out already I brush the ash and cigarette pieces from her couch ashamed and feeling more unathletic than ever.

(II)

I leave a couple hours before dawn. I walk quickly towards what is left of the sunset and find Mulberry. The sign is dilapidated but still reminds me of my parents' house. I have never tasted Jack Daniels but the familiar sign on the brick wall is intoxicating. I know I am headed the right way. Then I'm on campus. This isn't right. Mulberry was my landmark, my road, my point of reference. Not campus. I hear clamoring and instantly panic. Scared, I run in the opposite direction of my sunset. I weave through the edges of streets hoping for sidewalks. How is this so much more difficult the more clear-headed I am? I remember I was walking with her last time. And we came from the other side of the park. She wanted to find me a bicycle at Quinn's so I didn't have to walk anywhere. Instead I was too clumsy to find a bike that was any better than just walking. And with my poor navigation already I found myself more of a joke to her and the sales guys than I was comfortable with.

I pass the now quiet café almost half a day later. I made it this close without completely getting lost. Surely, I can find where we were. A park. A trail. Off this main road. No sidewalks. I finally find it and wander into the small urban forest. Picnic tables here and there along the way but, at first, I cannot find where the two main paths cross. Where we were attacked. Where she was attacked. Where the only survivor was me.

I killed a man. I killed several men. Several? Or one man twice? Damn it. There must be authorities after me. Would the kidnappers have called the police on me? Ruthless, they didn't even take a swing at me. Even as I took a knife to them. They are more evil than I, right?

Am I evil?

Does killing make me evil? I was defending her. I was defending her from here. This place. The bodies are gone but the stains remain. No police lines or investigators. No yellow tape to cross or curious reporters lurking about. I don't even know what it is that I am looking for. What type of clues can be found? How would I use them?

This place feels only strangely familiar. As if someone has told me about it in great detail. Someone else fought a great battle here for it does not feel as if it were me. Yet it was. A great battle lasting less than a minute. Or five. I don't know. And now I'm back and know not what I'm hunting. I fled and now I'm surrounded by guilt. I wish I would have stayed here with her even though she did not survive. Her blood is all that remains. She did not survive. Their blood accompanies hers. But this place has been cleared for the most part... by who?

She did not survive. That's all I know for certain.

My blood boils through my veins as though for the past decade I had been on a strict diet of caffeine, nicotine and no sleep.

I don't even smoke.

Only two days ago I was in her apartment waiting, hoping she would find half a day to spend with me. That half was today, and now there will not be another half with her. My day will forever be incomplete.

Car doors close nearby and I move to hide in a leaf-less tree. This damned winter cold will be the end of me if they have the sense to look upwards. I cannot climb trees. This is ridiculous. I'm too clumsy. I have no upper body strength. There is nowhere else to hide and if they are not the enemy then I will look completely foolish as the dolt climbing trees in the middle of a city park in the dead of an English winter.

They are definitely on a mission as they arrive and are thorough in their search. Except this tree, fortunately. These must be the same people who removed the bodies earlier as they show clear signs of familiarity of this area. Or just sheer confidence. Lack of fear. Unlike every emotion pouring through me. My nervousness and fear turn to anger and resentment. I want to know more. I must know more. Their faces are all I have to begin my revenge. For once in my life I feel I'm ready to stand up for myself.

For her.

They rummage through some bushes and never say a word to each other. They are quick to find what they are looking for, which is no evidence of a struggle at all. Surely, they know there is blood here, but it is on top of soil that a swift winter wind will hide soon. They leave, and I'm comforted that they never had any curiosity as to what evidence they might find up in the trees.

From here I cannot see the vehicle they return to. I can hear it drive off and feel safe enough to climb down. Once down I follow the same search pattern that they did and find nothing to compromise this area's innocence as a public park. Down four old stone steps to a grass circuit. I make the loop counting out 54 paces before I come back to the stone stairway.

There is nothing here that would prove anything happened here at all. They have wiped clean any chance I might have had to bring authorities here to help me.

There is nothing left here to feed my memory of her. I feel the tears come and I cannot move on. Actions from a little more than a half a day ago rush through my thoughts and I have no control over my mind forcing me to relive what happened.

How long ago? Not long ago now, but suddenly I remember it in clear detail:

Three of them walked quietly, silently towards us. From directly in front of us. They were not hiding nor did they come from behind. Their lack of concern to sneak up on us only made me feel as though violence was not on their mind. When I saw the first knife being pulled from under his coat I rushed in front of her to grab his hand and keep him from her. I kicked at another while the third walked right by me and grabbed her wrists. After being kicked that villainous cold-hearted devil didn't even so much as glance at me as he went after her. When he struck her in the face my rage erupted. I was still holding the forearm of the man with the knife and I slammed my forehead into his nose. The knife fell and he reached for his face and to fall gasping for his breath after I punched him solidly in the throat. He never recovered, which was fortunate for me as after I grabbed the knife from the ground I turned my back on him.

I did have a knife!

The man who struck her once struck her again as the other man swept her legs and took her to the ground. Anger rushed through my body.

I stabbed he who had hit her and felt the knife find its way between his ribs. As I twisted the weapon he coughed. I knew I had found a lung. I could not pull the knife out and as he grabbed the hilt and looked down I turned towards the third just in time to see him grasp her by the front of her throat and squeeze. Fear flooded her eyes as she looked at me one last time. Her gaze was that of how I would imagine someone drowning. Looking up through the clearest of water at me with the complete understanding that I could not help her and she must accept that her last breath had already been taken and she never had the slightest notion to have enjoyed it. He had crushed her throat with his bare hand and was grasping the back of her neck with his other hand in order to provide leverage and pressure to force the hand that had crushed her larynx further into her bleeding throat.

I struck out for his throat as I had with the first attacker. I was not so lucky this time. He was confident enough in her death that he finally looked at me. Before he could release his grip of her throat I brought my knee firmly into his groin. And then again so quickly he never had the chance to bring his blood-ridden hand near me. Instead he fell, and I kneed him again, this time in the chin. Rage took over and I pummeled him directly in the center of his face. Over and over again I followed him to the ground as he fell backwards. Hitting him so hard his face was falling in on itself with every punch. The cartilage in his nose ripped from the bone and back into his sinus cavity. My fists ached with every strike as he became more and more unrecognizable. He began to choke on his own face and all I could do was continue until I finally stopped my assault and turned towards her. She was no longer trying to find the ability to breath. She was no longer living.

I killed a man.

The man with the knife lodged into a lung began to rise and fell over again. Still struggling I left him there knowing he would not last long. I looked around hoping to find a way to help her. She had already perished. She had already lost all hope. They are still after her. Even in the grasp of death they are committed to killing her.

I must ensure they do not get away. In a fury I fight. I know now that I am no longer fighting for her life. She is gone. I am fighting for revenge. To the man on the ground with a knife in his lungs I reach first. I rip at the knife. I am instantly convinced that metal is somehow stronger than bone. He gasps and collapses. The same knife I plunge fully into his neck as he tries again to rise up. The force pushes him to the ground and I find myself following his limp body to the ground. I leave the knife.

I killed another man.

I realize now that there are only three. With his bloodied nose from a headbutt, the one left holding her does not seem to realize that she is dead. He looks as if she were his hostage. He is the first to look back at me and see that there is something beyond killing her. That I am here. That I am fighting back although she is already gone.

He holds her body as if I won't approach. And I approach.

7

He had no weapon. Only a grasp of her limp neck in the crotch of his arm and he squeezes tighter trying to persuade me away. And I kick. I kick harder than I've ever kicked before. I kick her in the ribs and graze off into his stomach. He's winded, but not from me. He drops her to the ground. As he starts towards me he kicks at my waist and I suddenly feel time slow.

The kick approaches and I consider if I deserve it. It will be the first blow I take in a fight. Ever. And for this fight, the first blow in a multiple murder from whomever wins this sudden one-on-one.

I watch her fall to the ground. I can feel the kick hit my waist.

She is lifeless and nothing makes that more evident to me than the way her arms remain useless as her head slams into the ground.

His arms are coming towards me. I cannot stop from watching her. She hits the ground and rebounds not once but twice from the concrete before I realize I'm falling myself. He steps in over me. My fury grows.

I grab his legs as he pummels my back. Paying no attention to my own head hitting the ground I plunge forward towards the earth. I miss the solid sidewalk and slam face-forward into the grass. He follows suit and loses his grip of my head after throwing punches hitting back first into the grass. I curl up, bring my legs up to my chest and I jump.

I have jumped too high with the heap of adrenaline I have amassed and he raises up to grab my legs. I still land on him, but awkwardly. We crash again to the ground. He head-butts my mid-section and I grab his head. I start to punch the back of his head futilely as he lifts me up. I anticipate a thrust towards the ground again and shift against his weight thrown forward. He stands and holds me up over his back like a 4-year-old over the back of his uncle. I grab his waste from behind as he tries to throw me. I pull tighter and grab for the thighs. I have no idea how to get my feet back on the ground.

He answers that question for me.

We begin to fall backwards. He obviously is aiming to pacify his part of the fall by landing on me. I allow it. He seems shocked by my lack of resistance and freezes for just a moment. Just long enough.

I push. The quickest push-up of my life and he slides easily to the side and I find myself rising above him.

He's easily bigger than I am.

Time that I thought was half as slow as possible slows again.

His clothes are well kept. He obviously works out. He has a sheath for not only a knife, but a gun. The knife has already been pulled. Possibly, hopefully, it has found its new home in the neck of his accomplice. The gun. Not in the holster. I never heard any shots. I never saw a gun. Did he not bring a gun?

He starts to rise. I hop and kick directly into his stomach. And I fall with my knee into neck. He raises his arms in defense but is too late. His strong defense becomes suddenly weak slamming helplessly against my ribs and falling to my thighs. His eyes roll.

He loses consciousness from the blow of my knee to the neck and his arms go limp. I stand up. He does not move. I look him over from head to chest to thighs to shoes. I don't know where to attack next. I am hopelessly devoted to hurting him more, but I cannot figure what will hurt the most. I settle on nothing and walk away.

I killed three men.

…And yet I am back in the same place of this tiny park. Impossible to walk away again. Impossible to grasp what happened to so many. To me. To her. In this place that has been restored to a park. Just a regular city park now.

I am here. I cannot stop replaying the circumstances that were just hours ago. It was only the last time I was here. I never want to be here again.

I would never need to be. And I walk away.

(III)

I am lost in this city. Hell, I'm lost in my own city. Always tied up on my computer, strapped into the information super-highway and always pretending that one day I will get out and find a way to be a man. I need resources. I need help. I need to at least give the appearance that I am not as lost as I am.

I am lost in this city.

At home I have always been a dreamer. I ensure that on any given day I can at least visualize a path to exactly where I want to be. For that day. A dot-com genius, an NFL place-kicker, a lotto winner. I've done it all within the course of twenty-four hours. Yet now I do not even know who I am nor would I want to be who he probably is being made out to be.

At home I don't even have mirrors that allow me to see anything below my waist. Actually, nothing even close to my belt line. I have likely invested in thousands of dollars' worth of workout videos and thousands more on top of that for workout equipment. Some table that I lay in once still haunts my guest bedroom and I don't even know if it's upright or flipped over. 4 different yoga mats rolled up and 4 times 4 yoga videos are sitting fully dust-ridden under my television. Tae-Bo. Billy Banks. Jane Fonda converted to DVD and color enhanced. Carmen Electra, yet somehow, I don't remember ordering that for fitness purposes.

The best video workout I ever had must have come from trying to keep up with David Byrne every time I watched The Talking Head's 'Stop Making Sense.'

Right now I would give anything for an empty stage and a lamp.

Here I have no dream. A dream implies a future and all I have is stuck in the past. The not too distant past. I am lost not only here in the physical but among any thought I have ever had. I know not which way to go. And there is absolutely no one to ask. No wiki to resource. No path to seek out and no books to find advice within. I have nothing and no skills to act upon. These streets are not empty. I can only hope that those here are as much tourists as I, or at least so native that however out of place I come across seems absolutely normal to them. This actually may not be such a bad place to be a foreigner.

I could possibly be of one of the largest minorities. Lost and ignorant. Someone to be brushed away into the afterthoughts of a stroll around town. I do not even know what part of town I'm in.

I dare not ask.

I board a bus as if I know exactly where it will lead me. I think I overpaid the fair but only the bus driver would know and she's not calling me out on it. The bus has a different atmosphere. More interesting characters than myself. I have been worried about carrying a backpack around but here it doesn't seem so out of place. Here I can think. Here I am not being followed. Here I believe I can find who I am supposed to be. Or find who I am now.

Here I stay until there is only one other person remaining on the bus. I figure I must get off before they do. It is an old man who had put many low denomination coins into the meter to board. I am certain by the bus driver's look that it must have ultimately been exact change too. When I finally get up he gets up too. I get off the bus at the rear door and he takes the long way to the front. How clever he is to bid farewell to the driver. I should have done the same.

He heads down the street in the same direction as the bus was headed but takes a quick right on the next street.

I follow.

He is headed towards the smell of machinery and salt water. The ports. I doubt highly that he works or lives there. Correction, takes up official residence there, so I think my curiosity is well placed. It's not long until he finds himself in front of a street vendor selling some sort of bread stuffed vegetable/meat combo. The vendor knows him by sight and shakes his head. A small debate occurs, and the bus-rider continues on his way.

Fortunately, I have money tucked away and I can score some dinner. I ask the same vendor for whatever is easiest, and he quips back with what I presume is an overpriced meal. I am not worried about it at the present and fork over his request. I cannot recall how long it has been since I ate. I cannot even recall the last thing I ate. So much so quickly. I take a bite and I am rushed immediately with an overwhelming sensation of guilt. My body's acceptance of sustenance is equally met with its retribution of life. I am an outcast within myself yet chewing has never been such an art. I look back towards the vendor with awe, but quickly turn back at the awkwardness I am starting to feel. He has no idea with what reverence I see him. I don't think I have ever had such a quick emotional attachment to someone. I am reminded with what infrequency I have dated and with what further infrequency I have found myself with a woman.

I am also dumbfounded at the extent my mind takes me having satisfied such a primordial necessity. To hell with him, I have food.

I have never been so hungry. With each bite I am savoring every calorie and every succulent morsel of food brought into this empty vessel of a man. Nothing has ever tasted so good or brought my senses to such delight. No wine or beer could ever be properly paired with this meal. My legs grow weak with nourishment. This is beyond finding the perfect Riesling and grilled Sea Bass. Lemon-peppered Prawns with Sauvignon Blanc. And even beyond a fresh nutmeg and peppered-bacon crusted beef tenderloin paired with a jammy, tannin intense Zinfandel.

This was sheer, classic hunger meets food.

I fall to a corner of the street and allow myself to pass out with no regret for the day at all.

(IV)

In my dream I am with her again. We are in a small room, an interrogation room, and she is accompanied by the three men who killed her. Only now they are on her side. For some reason she is questioning my motives for pursuing her.

"What brought you to the city?" she asks smooth and cold manner, which matched perfectly her impassionate expression.

My lips breathe "you" and my eyes scream "why?!"

As I am clammed up with thoughts of bewilderment she releases her companions to begin their assault on me. I cower. Not in defeat but rather in passion. With my face in my hands I take a deep breath awaiting the onslaught. I breathe out and look up. Rising to my feet I realize time has fallen to a crawl and I can suddenly evaluate every movement that is taking place. Ever so slowly they rush for me. Two of them around one side of the table and the third man directly over it. I kick the table as he leaps and the edge pounds his leading knee feeling the brunt of his own jump throb into his entire leg. The first man from the side has grabbed at my shoulder but I am able to make a quick punch to his midsection. Hard. Intently. Fully.

And I strike again with the same punch.

I pull my knee to find the groin of the man behind him and bring my foot down sharply against his shin and onto his foot. I drive my elbow back into the kidney of the first and slam the top of my head into the nose of the second. The man on the table has scurried over in time to shove me in rhythm with my headbutt. I stumble over an attacker and hit the wall. I turn to face him and gather my stance.

Only now she is there alone. No men. No table. No room. Just her. She is saddened. Holding a gun which she slowly raises to her head.

Her lips breathe "you" and her eyes scream "why?!"

I wake up in the streets before the dawn has come. I remember the passion of my dinner last night. And am then flooded by the horror of my dream. Disconsolate, I move into the street. I know nothing about where I am or what I am going to do. No person is around, just the low hum of the ports that never sleep. It's quiet, and peaceful, and so fucking disheartening I would rather be back in my dream.

I look back to where I slept and start to look for landmarks. A sign or a lamppost or a color... something. For a moment I am determined to note this area like a parking spot in a giant shopping mall or a trailhead in Yellowstone or the obscure folder on your computer buried deep within other folders that you do not wish to name with words. Then I realize that I am not in need of such security. No finite place should hold my return. I am no longer someone who should find such solace in any place. Or with any person. Or suddenly even with myself.

I must find a way to find who they were. Why they did what they did. And what she was that was beyond me.

Obviously, there is some secret she held that has jolted me from any semblance of a normal life. Worst case scenario is that I am a fugitive witness of a murder whose story would only make me seem guilty. Best case they have accomplished their mission, she is gone, my hiding out is futile and I return home after a mild vacation.

My passion merely two days ago was getting her to notice me, now I am convinced just as much that I have to clear her name as well as mine. I know I am no hero and I know she would only laugh at me, but now that she's gone there's no one whose laughter would mean anything to me. Insulting or not. There's no one who could convince me of whatever my place in life should be. I suddenly feel like I can find my own path, as vague as it may be now, it is my own. No more trying to compare my life to others and no more wondering 'what if'.

I killed a man.

I killed three.

And God help me I am scared to death, but I am going to walk this road as though it were all of the answers to all of the questions I could come up with.

Who were they? There were obviously hired. Obviously? Yes, had to have been.

If they were the ones who needed her dead, then why would they be ok with death themselves? It's never the minds of a terrorist cell that commit suicide, just the hearts. Those who have convinced others that there is a cause worth fighting for and worth dying for are not the ones who will die, but rather the ones that will live to see the cause fulfilled. Like any Aries and their many projects and their many passions, they have passed it on to ensure its life and its fulfillment, but they will never be there at the end of any war they start. Whoever wanted her dead, whoever felt her death was necessary and whoever had the knowhow to convince others that her death was more important than their own life, is still out there and they have only completed another piece in whatever puzzle they have certainly created.

Who was she? More than anyone I thought she was before. For so long she was so much. She had my attention at any given time. She never wanted it. She could convince me of anything. She never tried. She never was going to be attainable for me. She never wanted to be. But maybe she did like me. Perhaps she actually found a friendship with me that forced her to push me away and like a fool I pursued stronger. It's possible she did like me. Maybe she never wanted whatever it was that she had found. Maybe she never found anything. Maybe she was a creator. Someone who had developed or prophesized. She could have been anything for them. She was brilliant. She was beautiful. She was obviously more than they could handle.

Or maybe she wasn't who they were actually after. She was definitely surprised by them. She didn't have a look about her like she knew what was happening. She wasn't a skilled fighter. She didn't carry any weapons. She could have just been a college student mistaken for one of their own.

But then she wasn't hiding anything from me. Her intentions were true to the way she was living them.

I am still nothing.

If I am going to solve this for any reason at all I have got to account for what is going on.

Think.
Think.
Think.
Where am I? What do I have? What do I need?

Here I have my anonymity. Here I have only one focus. Here I have time.

I do not know where to go, so perhaps I'll just see what happens here. I do not know what to seek, so perhaps I'll see what comes to me. I know that if I go back into the world that I let go of any chance for discovery. Going home would be letting go, and I am not ready to let go. I need to become something new. I need to become ears and eyes and memories. I need to find and seek and understand. Where am I? I am in the same city that she was. Staying here is my option. There would be no better start than here. This city, these streets, these ports. I must make this my home. Of course, this makes the most sense.

PORT OUT

The left side of a sailing vessel, facing away from the shore.
The view of endless possibilities from the shore out into the sea.

(I)

Behind me there will be a great path that stands
before me now.
I will walk the stones that only I can walk
And that only I will turn to see behind me.
In front of me there is a great path that behind me
is soon to know.

(II)

Patience. Clarity. Safety.

I get the feeling of security amongst all the bustle of these ports
and the streets nearby. Like being one of the crowd keeps me from
standing out. I am most definitely lost, but I have kept my head down
and walked like I have known where I was going and pretty much
have been ignored. I noticed some of my future neighbors nestled
behind shops, some on alleyway entrances and others closer to the
docks. That is where I have found myself mostly. Shelter comes from

an old awning and I am enclosed between two old shipping crates, enormously long, but I have about a 3-foot width and 10-foot depth to call my own. No evidence of a previous owner, and not so secluded that I seem to be hiding, only living and amongst those you wish could be ignored a little better.

Front page of yesterday's paper has a murder case: 22-year-old female knifed in her own home.

"Continued on B7: Knifed"

B7 is hardly an article, and it doesn't mention any names. I doubt the writer knows anything. He does not know she wasn't just murdered the day before yesterday. What I don't doubt is that it is her. Also, that because she was found in her home, that tells me it wasn't any authority that found her in that park. And I am sure the 3 guys that killed her were "found" somewhere else if they were even ever found at all.

I can picture a future B7 now, and I can picture a reference to one killer. Likely a friend. Likely me. Specifically. Maybe not ever to be put in print, but on the minds of those that found her there.

I have got to find them first.

I have not dared to tap back into the computer world or even search the internet. After all the blood had dried and I could pick enough off me to look like any normal homeless person, I made a bus trip. I connected to four different buses and ensured I randomly chose my path but memorized the connections for my return trip. The first route I selected went by the Medical School and right into her neighborhood. I did not see anything or learn anything new. Just finding methods to blend in.

At the turning point of this venture I found an ATM machine and removed the maximum. In the restroom of a Fish & Chips shop I taped the money envelope to my thigh. Fried foods tasted so good but did not settle too well. I made my way back to the ports and my 3' by 10' with a fresh newspaper in hand.

For the most part I sit and listen. I will panhandle quietly at times to ensure I fit into the scene, but I am fishing for information rather than coins. When I feel I am at the top of my game, clean and confident, I wonder around the Marina. Here I watch the sailboats and decipher the wind. I used to find my favorite websites and contemplate the HTML code that made them do what they did. Now I watch sailors navigate each page as the wind pushes little 0s and 1s into their canvassed sails. I have watched patiently enough to see the frustrated amateurs think they have positioned their sails perfectly only to continuously align and realign. It reminds me of my impatient mother on her new laptop clicking and reclicking the mouse not realizing the page is simply taking its time to load. I get such a kick out of seeing the wind pick up suddenly and nearly launch the puzzled sailors from the bow of their little boats.

The tides are peaceful to me, even amongst the bustle of a dock. I try to stay away from being noticed too much in one place but the draw of watching the sails and the tides is more captivating than any keyboard, screen and broadband modem. I have accepted that I do not have a path, and feel I am adequately hidden here. When I want to contemplate my situation, I walk. When I want to forget my situation, I watch the passing ships. When I want to do neither, I exercise.

I have never exercised so much in my life. Just one week's worth of this much movement I have lost at least 8 pounds, half my gut and have found a spring in my step. It builds confidence. And although I have nowhere or nobody to show my confidence to, I can feel it growing.

Meanwhile, the wind fascinates me. I stand facing out towards the Irish Sea and embrace the blowing breeze upon my face. Salt heavy in the wind. I close my eyes and listen to it whisper to me in stereo. I know it intimately now and know when it is screaming far away at others and I know when the wind wishes to speak only to me.

All day, every day is a long time when it is all you have.

I see the white crests upon shallow waves and look ahead on the water's path to see which sail will benefit the most. I have been humored by the unaware who try fighting a headwind to get to shore, and I have slept well after watching the most confident of machismos perch themselves upon the bow and prepare their skyward chests for an epic battle against the wind only to turn back puzzled seeing their sails flap helplessly against a sullied mast.

I have stood in awe of a crew numbering greater than a dozen scurrying to trim full sails in unison. A captain barking orders to any able-bodied sailor who begins to follow the command before he is even been told. Watching a sail seemingly inhale the wind like a drowning man who suddenly finds himself breaking from his watery grave.

The water and the wind tell a great tale. Their dance is impressive and often intimidating. It is mesmerizing watching them become as one. It is humorous watching sailors of old and new trying to take charge of the wind and master the waters. I have never been out on a boat, but I imagine the difficulty only grows the farther away from the shore they go.

I wonder if I can sail.

(III)

I wake up in my little crevasse of the world and note it is not quite dawn. I want to think that I am so in tune with the day that I am waking with the sun's first showing, but then I hear the garbage trucks rattling in an alleyway behind me. I sit up and lean against the thick metal container I call home. I can feel the envelope of money against my leg and try to calculate how much is in there.

In fact, I think there is more now than I maxed the ATM with. Not much more, but more is significant nonetheless. These homeless guys don't have it too bad.

I pick up the newspaper from two days ago that is filed in the corner of my real estate and head out on my new routine to find yesterday's paper. I have been living in the world's shadow, behind

by just a day. I cannot find any information pertinent enough for me
to worry about news much quicker than that most days. The stock
market does not pertain to me and I can see some of the swings based
on the amount of business done in restaurants nearby. What amazes
me is the change in business the ports show about 3 to 5 business days
after I see a swing in the stock market or a drop or rise in the Euro.

You see a lot on the ports within just two weeks.

There is not much news to find regarding the American Dollar
or the Yen, but when it happens I see very little significance in the
day to day of these ports.

I imagine it is like watching the crests of water and following
the wind here close to the shore. Battling the market and following
its swings and changes is bound to be more difficult out on the open
sea. A subtle change in the direction of the wind here could cause a
drift of epic proportions in the middle of the Irish Sea, but also could
wither down and be masked by a colossal wave stemming from an
underwater earthquake in the middle of the Atlantic.

I have too much time on my hands. I should find a way to wash
my hair. It's nearly double in length from how short it was when I
arrived in this country. I cant see it yet, but I can feel it.

Instead I walked past the docks on my way to gather the leftover
newspaper from yesterday when a man calls out to me.

"Sir! Sir! Hey boss, over here! Can you help me out?"

I walk to him and his Irish accent. Apparently, I have failed
to look as homeless as I would like. Or he is just not interested
in anything more than a helping hand. He is aboard a one-mast
sailboat. The mainsail set and the headsail poised halfway up the
mast. I had noticed other crews rig their sails this way when they were
shorthanded, but never by just one man.

"No crew this morning?" I call out as I untie the rope tethering
him to the dock.

"No, they didn't show, and I've got to get out before that storm
cloud steals my wind." He said pointing towards the Northwest sky.

Pushing the boat a little for him, "You'll have a decent gust here in about 20 minutes or so as it passes…"

"Absolutely, but I want to make sure I catch that 'decent gust' about one knot out from here and let it carry me to Dublin." He looked back at me with an odd look on his face as the boat started to pick up speed. Yelling now, "What's your name, boss?"

"Robert!" I yelled back instinctively and immediately returned the same odd grimace he had just given to me. As he nodded with acknowledgement I knew he was remembering my name as though it were a license plate on a car that had just hit his new Beamer in the parking lot. I returned the favor and decided that sailboat and Dublin were not to escape my memory.

I made my way two blocks over to the front of an office building where I would find the news from yesterday reported, read and dropped back to the earth.

The paper is still wrapped in the plastic bag it was delivered in. The business owner it was intended for has yet again left it where it initially lay and taken today's paper. I am amused at the symbiosis we have had. They walk out at some point and pick up the paper. They remove the sports section from the paper and then bring that paper back to the yard the next morning, drop the old paper, bag and all, right back where the delivery person threw it. I wonder how many papers would be piled up here on the front walk if it were not for me. I imagine their joy of having not to worry about the paper equals my joy of not having to deal with the sports section.

I have always read the entire paper, or watched an entire newscast when tv was available, including the sports which I never followed. It always baffled me that they could get away with a cross-contamination of analogies. I still think it just illustrates the lack of wit they have when they reference a point-guard of a basketball team as the quarterback. May as well call a homerun a touchdown. In fact, I think they have a time or three.

I glance at the headlines while walking back. I am suddenly thankful that North and South Korea are testing their border as I get to the second most important article of the front page.

"3 More Found Murdered in Their Homes"

The word *more* is the most troubling to me. The implication of something previous. A murder in someone's home.

More *lies*.

The sun breaks over the horizon and finds me like a spotlight. The breeze picks up and whittles away at my confidence. I do my best to scan the article but all I can deduce is that the story is fabricated. Then I see her name.

> *"…similar stab wounds as the recently murdered student, Samantha Atwater, who was also found in her home less than two weeks ago. Authorities say these killings may be by the hand of the same killer."*

Killer. Singular. Not dead killers who killed her. Not case closed. Not murder in the park. Not anything about the truth. The truth that only I know. Even those that moved the bodies did not know the whole truth. Someone is happy that the truth is not out there. Someone has more influence than I do. Someone can paint a picture on a canvas that only I have seen unpainted. Well, myself and four who were recently killed. Apparently by the same hand.

My hand likely. I wonder how long until they say it. One day I imagine I will read my name along the list of names killed, only I will not be dead with them. It is the only logical thing I can see them doing. Making me the point. The fingered. The fugitive killer.

"continued B1, Slain in Homes"

And then there it is at the bottom of B1. Front page of the second section in yesterday's paper. My name.

> *"The Parents of Atwater say the student had an American visitor, Robert Garin Carlyle, visiting her recently. Carlyle's own family has reported him missing and confirmed his trip to England. Carlyle is wanted for questioning by the Merseyside Police. Anyone with information about Carlyle or his whereabouts should contact..."*

Frustrated with anger I forget that I am even walking still. I fold the paper back perfectly, only now the section that will make me famous is on the front. I sheath it back into the plastic and concentrate. Only I do not have anything to debate. The facts are there in front of me. She is dead. Three more are dead. I am missing. They want to talk to me. Those are the facts and that is all someone had to provide. The police can mark me all they want now. Beyond those facts the story does not matter. Everything that is in the paper that was not part of her dead, them dead, me missing, gives all the speculation needed to commit me to every reader's list of criminals.

Murderers.

Murderer.

Fugitive.

Killer.

Me.

There has got to be some information for me here. I have got to find who it was that moved the bodies. That took her back to her flat. That positioned them all to be discovered.

What did my family tell them? The truth? I can only imagine.

What do they suppose my motive is?

I pass the docks where I gave my name out for the first time since and I look out as far as I can. I see the boat. It is slowing with the dying southward wind and all the sails near the dock have already fallen loosely. A couple curious sailors are looking around hoping for signs while the few captains out at this time have poised their sails for the change in wind to soon arrive. The vessel pointed towards Dublin has yet to come to a complete stop when he has already completed a change in his sails from zig-zagging through a headwind and is readied to catch a sudden tailwind from the shore.

He loses no time and catches the wind's change perfectly. Full speed towards the Irish Sea. On a sailboat usually manned by at least three trained men he moves effortlessly. He will make the trip to Dublin before lunch time.

I wonder if he has yesterday's paper tucked under his arm.

(IV)

As everything else has been predictable I presume that my photo will appear in the paper soon. I take comfort in having a beard now, having lost nearly 20lbs in the past month, my driver's license from home being 7 years old and no one here knows me. Also, considering everything was derived from a frame-job, not all the pieces are perfectly laid out and detectives are still trying to put together a puzzle ill-formed to begin with.

So I hope, at least.

In the sense of predictability, I also presume that I must take my usual routes and be subtly seen as I always have been. Subtly by everyone except the one captain. He who sails alone towards Dublin. This will allow me to continue picking up my late paper. Although now I have some good reason to get the paper a little sooner.

I don't know, authorities are not prevalent out here. Most of these people are wealthy and do not need policing. Well, they do not need their day-to-day policed, let's just say that.

I catch the bus and travel passed campus. I now know both bus drivers who run this route during the weekdays, not by name or greeting, just by sight. It is quite comforting getting on the bus. Like catching the base of the light-pole that served as base during the neighborhood hide-and-seek game. I look out the window and it feels like I am holding onto that cool metal cylinder again. Spotting other kids hiding in bushes or standing defiantly in the middle of the street. Waiting to make a run for the very pole I stood next to or for "it" to start chasing them in an open asphalt playing field.

I am safe here. At least I feel that way. Part of the transiting public saving the world one tank of gas at a time. Shielded from the elements by a single sheet of glass ready to pop out with the pull of a bright red handle. We stop before every railroad crossing and, as long as Newton's theories hold up, we would be victorious in any car collision.

I do my utmost to never be the one who requests a stop. I like when I see someone waiting already at the stop ahead. Or a familiar face I know will get off at certain stops. I am also not opposed to exiting the transit one stop before or one after and making the short walk to where I need to be. After all, time can only be good to me.

On this trip that is exactly what I am left to do. I pass my intended stop as no one else apparently wanted it and no one was waiting there to board. Passing the stop by nearly a full mile I got off with a crowd. A newsstand was on the corner just across from the bus stop. I overpaid for a paper and didn't get so much as a "hey buddy" from the vendor.

Normally I avoid cafes and take to eating from a street vendor. Today was no exception, but I need to find some sort of common ground from the two options. I try with all my might to ignore the *"Liverpool University Murders"* headline on the front page. I walk patiently towards a falafel vendor who sets up awkwardly on the sidewalk near a couple of benches. The awkwardness plays to my favor today as he has hoped consumers would take advantage of the nearby seating to enjoy his product instead of just passing by, but consumers do not want to sit that close to the vendor. They especially do not want to sit anywhere near a homeless man.

To tell the truth I look a little better than a panhandler today though. Scruffy for certain, but the humidity has tamed my straight hair and it lay down conservatively. Mostly conservatively. Also, a paper in hand always seems to give casual observers some sense of sophistication. A cup of coffee would have sealed the sophisticated citizen motif, but falafel-guy does not sell coffee. You would think a Middle Eastern dish, even as street food, would be accompanied by a Turkish coffee. This guy wasn't even Middle Eastern though. Falafel-guy was French, the best I could tell, and must have had parents of different descents considering his complexion. Whatever the case may be, he could pass for whatever he wanted to, at least second generation, and by all means should have at least had some over-roasted French coffee.

I sit and read words like "alleged" and "unconfirmed" and "so-called" all the while looking at a photo of myself. It was taken at Daytona Beach. I am happy that this was the photo used. It meant my parents submitted it for my vanishing. They probably were clueless about the words surrounding the photo, at least when they chose it. It portrayed me with them, they were edited out, when I had taken them to the beach to celebrate my new job. I was about 55 pounds heavier than I am now. Even when I started this trip I was thinner than that photo.

Still fat, just not as fat as the photo.

This bought me more time. That and people who saw the photo would assume I looked like that yesterday and I could not possibly have grown a solid beard that quickly.

At least this was all that I hoped. And my hopes were what were going to help me keep my patience moving forward. Logic and perception where my best of friends.

Information was a little better in this article. It listed Sam as an up and comer at the University, which was arguable, and most importantly it gave some background on the three men. It posed them as individuals, seemingly not ever even knowing each other, and as businessmen. Professionals and pillars of the community.

In fact, from my perspective, a little too wordy for anyone, even if it were partially true. The fluff was likely there to make me seem more devious. This gave me goals. I could break down an imposter with the right information. I just needed the information. The article was clever enough to have given me the addresses in which the bodies were found.

It was time to consult a map. I had maps of the city but only used them to find where I was.

It was time to find something else. It was time to gather information about this city.

There was not a good map to be found at the newsstand on the corner, and I did not want to board the bus where I got off anyway. I walked some ways and found my way back onto the bus. I suddenly felt like a celebrity with the knowledge I read. That and my photo in the paper. But I was ignored with a slight disgust just like every other day. I sat with my paper underarm and my eyes out towards the trees hunting for children hiding.

Suddenly base was not as secure as it had been, and the metal lightpole was cold to the touch. I closed my eyes and counted the stops until I was back at the docks.

I arrived farther south than I had left and did not pass the same way I went out. For the first time my strategy paid off. My previous path was blocked by three uniformed officers and one frustrated sailor pacing near the edge of the dock. I slowed my pace and shuffled a bit looking solemnly towards the ground. I made my way to the entrance of my alleyway and picked up my pace to go file my new paper with the others. I would sift through and try and decipher some clues the writer may have left later tonight, but I needed to know what was bringing the police to the normally quiet docks.

I hurried back to the public sector before I started my shuffle again. I feigned a disgruntled look at the sun and sat on a curb just out of earshot. I put a blank piece of cardboard out in front of me. I never thought to write on it but I thought the words would not matter to anyone who was giving money anyway. I really did not want to lie to them, but I would happily accept their charity.

There were enough people at the docks to make me feel safe enough to not be questioned, but from the man's position he was familiar with that sector of the dock. Exactly where I helped loose a sailboat yesterday morning. Exactly where I gave my name to a man headed to Dublin.

A man sailing in a hurry on a boat all alone.

A man who was quite good at what he was doing.

A man who knew me now and likely was suspicious of how much I knew him.

If he were ever to return.

As I put the pieces of this small investigation together I realized I knew too much. I was in a poor position for my situation and did not want to push it. I had enough to worry about than to add boat theft accomplice to my recent resume.

(V)

I looked over all of the papers as I was tucked away in my little nook. There was enough daylight left to read them all slowly. They painted me as the boyfriend I wish I was. They put her GPA in the latest article two times. One of the men was a grocery store executive and the other two were public servants, working for different members of Parliament. One tied to Liverpool and the other to Wirral. True or not, they wanted to portray the men as separate individuals. All three. And her, as a fourth victim unrelated to the three men.

For the community it meant there was a killer amongst them with no motive. No pattern to his actions and could strike anywhere upon anybody. For me it meant they were trying too hard to separate their lives and all I had to do was find their connections. Who were these men and what was their common ground? It may also be plausible to find their supposed co-workers and illustrate a lack of personal knowledge.

I lean back against my impenetrable fortress and contemplate strategy to unfurl their plot against me. Finally having information, good or bad, is overwhelming and I can feel myself drifting off before the sun has even set.

I fall asleep.

I dream that I am back on the bus but it is not moving. I am the only one on it and get up from the back to exit. The windows are dark and I cannot see out. My security has been removed with the simple act of taking my view away. I open the door to a blinding daylight.

As I step off the bus I notice I am clean shaven and dressed in new clothes. Hoping to catch my reflection in a window I turn back towards the bus. It is no longer there. I am on a dock looking out over water that reaches to the horizon. Three sails off in the distance are full and geared towards me. Newspapers are blowing in a strong wind around me and taunting me with their headlines. Passersby are all reading the papers and looking at me between paragraphs. More people start coming from every direction.

Their numbers are growing.

Their looks are lingering.

I turn back towards the water to find the sailboats. The sails are growing larger against the water.

As the wind picks up around me I can see the small waves against the shore have lost their drive towards land. The wind will be too much to navigate against soon. I start to panic. I want to be on a boat. I want to test my observations. I want to get away from these people.

Their numbers grow.

The wind blows heavily towards the waters.

Still holding newspapers, they begin to gather around me. The boats have nearly come to a halt against the wall of air keeping them from the shore. Each boat has but one sailor. They all three stall their boats. Two are forced into a retreat and the third navigates itself stagnant facing the wind. I give in to their loss and turn to face the crowd behind me.

I am forced to lean towards the masses of people gathering as the wind picks up.

They are too close now for comfort and I am expecting to be rushed. Why must they be so tedious in their attack? What are they waiting for? I contemplate attacking first and then I see swarms follow in line behind them. They incorporate the entire dock. File after endless file. They have all read and they all know.

They have all read.

They all know the truth.

They stand tall and brace against the wind to their backs. The more that fill in the calmer the wind becomes. I turn to see the zig-zagging of an accomplished sailor headed into the wind. He is picking up speed as the wind is brought further under control by the gathering crowd on the waterfront. His path becomes straighter and straighter until he arrives with precision stopping just before the dock. Port out.

The wind has come to a stop as it is walled against thousands of people. They have allowed the boat to arrive.

I look back and see the assurance of those gathered. I step onto the boat and waver with uncertainty in my first step aboard. I look at the boat thief and he nods with authority. I pause and step carefully aboard growing my sea legs stronger with each step.

The crowd begins to disperse, and the wind catches the sails in full. I step back within the boat and watch as he trims the sail to guide us at full speed towards the horizon. All I see is water and I care not to turn back.

THE ISLE O' DREAMS

The songs, the emotion and the inspiration of the people of Ireland.
Irish dreams? Or dreams of being Irish?

(I)

"Curtis!"

From a barstool, the boat thief turns his head slightly and presents one eye towards the man who'd called his name.

"Curtis!" is called again across the small bar as a large man lifts himself up from a table. He leans into his first step to gain momentum and finds fluidity in his movement. His concentration on getting vertical conveniently allowed for short-term memory loss as he called once again, "Curtis!"

Curtis Scott could feel the warmth from the whiskey on the man's breath even from his seat at the end of the bar. Anyone with half a brain in this bar knew Curtis was a thief, but it took Bradly O'Sheel and his "keep 'em coming" attitude to call him out on it publicly.

"Was that a Pearson 424 I saw you coming in on this morning?" None of which was audibly decipherable, least alone the numbers. "My dad and I saw two of those in Hawaii, but never sailed by just *one man*. Is that a Pearson?"

Curtis was purposely loud enough to be overheard by two other people, neither of which was O'Sheel, "I haven't been on a boat in weeks."

"Where did you bring it in from? Is there somebody who already has bought it from you? Did you sell it yet?" his speech was growing in clarity with every step. He was gaining his composure as if he had a MagLite with fresh Ds shining in his face, "You're the only one I know who is crazy enough to take a boat like that across the sea by himself."

Cooly finishing off the last of his beer Curtis turned and reached an arm out, palm upwards, to greet his friend. "Now Bradly, the last thing I need is for you to be looking to start a war with me in the middle of this bar."

"No one here listens to me. They never have." He leaned in to where only the two men could hear each other, "Next time don't cut me out okay?"

"I didn't cut you out, friend. Guy from Egypt wants this exact boat and wanted nobody to know anything about it."

"So it is a Pearson 424, then?" O'Sheel used his hip against the bar like a kickstand, "How'd you locate it?"

"The boat's *now-previous* owner was bragging about having the only one in the…" Curtis caught himself even before he had to bite his own tongue, "Well, the only one."

He watched O'Sheel nod his understanding and set his empty glass down just in time to be met with a fresh beer and another shot of whiskey. Bradly punched the bar top twice looking at the barkeep to give his thanks before twisting his way into the seat next to his friend. Both men found comfort facing straight ahead at the 18" non-HD television crammed between the backup Scotch bottles. They embraced the silence between them as only thieves could.

Bradly O'Sheel and Curtis Scott had done enough jobs together to know each of their capabilities. O'Sheel also understood the importance of a solo mission by Curtis. The man to his left, the man who learned to sail on his father's boat as a child, had been gone for nearly 6 weeks. It was not like Curtis to be away from Dublin for more than 9 or 10 days. He could sail his way around, especially across the Irish Sea, better than most people could get around with a motorboat. This was the first time he ever mentioned anything about Egypt.

Bradly and Curtis used to be equals on a sailboat. Considered masters of the wind by Bradly's father and his troupe at early ages, they could out-sail any other group of teenagers throughout high school and made some decent gambling wages doing so. Sailing teams seemed to never catch on to the advantage two men had versus four men, at least not in their adolescence. Curtis went on to join crews and be a boat hand. Bradly's dad insisted on college where, although he graduated eventually, he seemed to only put on weight and grow taller. His size kept him from joining Curtis and his life on the sea, but his new-found business skills kept the two with plenty of pocket change. Bradly always knew who was looking for the right purchase, the going rate for hot sea crafts, and Curtis had a knack for supplying the demand.

Bradly's father was in a position to be Harbormaster for the ports of Dublin, but his lack of Navy experience held him back. He was still afforded many privileges, including appointing Bradly to a high title, low responsibility management position. Bradly made more money off Curtis each year than he did from his base pay. His financial struggles were limited only to ensuring his lifestyle was seen to be within his means.

Thanks to his father, Curtis only "worked" when he had to.

"Have you been to Egypt before?"

"No…" His excitement was honest, but his reaction was one of disdain. Curtis had done countless trips East and West but had never really been South. Not Egypt-South. Never been into the Mediterranean. He had not even considered it before now. "I'll be headed down in a couple days."

"Speak any Egyptian?"

Curtis looked at his drunk friend with amusement. "I'm fluent." He shot over as he took a long pull on his beer finishing it off. He pushed the glass forward along the bar and savored the hoppy aftertaste.

Taking a break from whatever was normally going on in his mind, Bradly put thought to his words, "They speak English in Egypt?"

Curtis Scott nodded with confirmation. A small smile between friends acknowledged Brad's tendency to let his beer do his thinking. The bartender arrived with two fresh pints and placed them on two new coasters. Brad made the last quarter of his beer seem as though it were the first liquid he had found after a week in the desert. With giddy he smiled and nodded his thanks to the bartender who was not even looking anymore.

Fighting his own tendency to talk too much about subjects he shouldn't, Curtis started to bite his tongue but missed, "I'm supposed to meet someone outside of Gibraltar before I go through." He paused realizing some relief in just having someone else know his secrets.

"If you need any help getting through Gibraltar let me know." Bradly felt good knowing now he shared some of the criminal bourdon of his good friend.

"The way he spoke was so vague, I don't even know if I'll be going through to the Mediterranean." Curtis finally grabbed for his new beer and pulled it closer, almost ready to take a taste.

"If you need any help." Bradly concluded as he downed his whiskey shot.

They both turned towards the television and knew no more about the subject would be spoken. Curtis looked at the full pint in front of him and held on as though it anchored him to the bar. He reached out with his left and gently touched the edge of the cardboard coaster suctioned to the bottom of his glass. Free at last from being tethered to the bar top, the vessel that was Curtis Scott drank from the anchor of brew in his hand. It was filled with the same excitement and nervousness he found with his maiden voyage.

(II)

He ran his hand along the edge of the boat. The two first fingers on his left hand touched all 42 feet and the next 4 inches of the Pearson 424. It was off white with light pine-colored wood accents.

The bottom was deep green, making it look as though it sat quite shallow in the water. As the boat bobbed gently in the Dublin Ports he could feel the vast displacement the enormous underbelly of the boat made in the water.

Moving soft, but powerful waves against the port's pillars, the P424's strength was evident. This was a big boat. Dominant. The mast stretched high with the main sail down. It was white reinforced aluminum and during the day could shine brighter than the reflected sun. It was the color of a breaking wave near the shore. The ocean's spray against an immobile rock.

The random ringing of the pullies against the metal mast and the slow flapping of the sails made Curtis feel at home.

And he was.

He boarded the stolen vessel that, for the time being, was his. Starboard home he was at the bow of the sailboat. He walked along the port side touching each winch as if he had installed them all himself. Even a little drunk, he walked along the deck though the boat was a concrete fixture welded at its core to Ireland's love for St. Patty's Day; unwavering. He ran a finger over the cold metal of the steering wheel and gripped it at the top. Slowly he turned the wheel a quarter turn. With no sails up, there was no movement to be noted from moving the rudder.

Walking down the few steps into the cabin he turned and flipped on the light switch with ease. He did not care for the burgundy accents to the pine-colors, but he had to note it was chosen by someone with some cash. Somebody loved this boat, or at least loved the idea of this boat. It was too clean inside for a true sailor to have owned this. Either that or it was remodeled the day before he stole it.

He opened the refrigerator and took note of the few staples he did not already pillage for his lunches. He thought about his street-worn new buddy Robert back in Liverpool. By now news of this missing boat were bound to be all over the ports in England, he just wondered if the authorities had been alerted to the fact it was very likely here in Dublin. If they found it here in Dublin there would be no question who had taken it. He did not expect anyone to take a fall for him, but he knew no one would be the first to report him. At least no one from Ireland.

He pulled a can of Cain's IPA from the fridge and popped the top. It marked his conclusion to stay on the boat that night. He sat on the bed and set the beer down on the counter nearby. Worry started to set in.

"Robert" he said to himself as he lay down to sleep. A full can of beer fizzled loudly easing him to sleep like a cheap recording of ocean waves.

STARBOARD HOME

The right side of a sailing vessel, often close to the shore.
The view from sea looking towards solid ground.

(I)

No matter how close to the water I was, it always seemed so far away. Calling to me as though it were in a previous life. Or a future one.

The authorities never asked me about the stolen boat. Turns out they were about as interested in the theft as you would expect them to be. Good for me, bad for the boat owner. I gathered newspaper clippings together and put them in order of their printing:

Murder.
Murder of local college student.
College girl and three others found murdered.
Killer at large.
Samantha Atwater, the details of an innocent college girl murdered in her home.
Robert Garin Carlyle, posing as a friend to Samantha, on the loose. What is his motive? Will he kill again?

They portray my intelligence through my web-design and computer programming background. The make sure it sounds pretty creepy, too. As though I have been stalking her against her will. I do not even believe the fabrications are that far of a stretch. She was all I had to drive me in life, and she tried gently to keep me away. I sat in front of my computer most days delaying work until it was needed. My idea of a productive day was putting the cleanest clothes I had into the dryer and trying to get as many wrinkles out as possible. I would head into the office and parade around talking about the latest webisode of 1Up or a Network Security Podcast by Martin McKeay, but truth be told, I had only caught up for the previous week to look smarter than I was.

I had always been resourceful.

It had always worked.

And now interviews with my coworkers paint me as more of a psychopath than I would have ever imagined. They all thought I was a flop. An overweight spaz who only wanted to talk about himself. I actually just talked to seem like I had something to say, it never really was about myself. There was nothing there to talk about. I even made her seem like she was more than a pen-pal, even when we were younger.

Samantha had moved onto my block when I was twelve. She was ten and her family bought the house four months before they moved in. It was an old neighborhood in the middle of town and ours was the, soon-to-be, smallest house on the block. We only lived there because my mother's family had for nearly 40 years. Now our neighbors were people who had money and were moving in for the nostalgic inner-city life. They wanted to live in an old neighborhood, but they all insisted on having a modern house. A large modern house.

Other mothers in the neighborhood always told my mom how great her house was. That it was what made this neighborhood special. Many of them even made her offers to buy it. She always declined. Mom loved her house and was working her hardest to pay the property taxes each year. She rode the bus to work and stayed in the front yard most of the time.

Maybe that was why I never wanted to be outside. I loved my mother but hated to be seen with her. I spent my days inside trying to master Penguin Land on my Sega Genesis. My friends at school didn't even know their system had it built in and always wondered where I got the game. I told them I had made it.

Then Sam arrived.

She was half a foot shy of 5 foot at only 10 years of age, and although she would never gain more than 8 more inches of height, for this 12-year-old she was perfect. I envied her playing basketball all day. Her red hair matching the color of the ball and her pale skin matching the backboard. And green eyes that matched nothing besides each other. She was taller and faster than all the other kids in the neighborhood and I wanted to be her friend. At 12 there wasn't anything sexual I desired towards her, in fact that never really developed into a desire for me, but I did want to be known as her friend. And I tried so hard.

On the days my mother stayed inside, or weeded the backyard, I went out to try my hand at basketball. She was always willing to let anyone play. Unselfish competitor. Even if she lost, or purposely lost as I'm sure she did against me, she had this confidence leaving the game as though she had gained more from the game than you did.

She always talked about sports, and I about television and the newest computer software. We never really talked to each other, just kind of next to each other.

Adjoining neighborhood children would end up on our street to play hide-and-seek. The light-pole in the middle of the street was the best base for the 'seeker'. It was the highest point on the street and posed as a great lookout point. Also, all the hiders, from both directions on the street, were running uphill to get to base. Considering there could be up to twenty kids playing any given day, any advantage to the seeker was needed.

I always tried to follow Sam to her hiding spot. My clumsiness usually gave us away and we would have to run. Her towards the light-pole-base and me just away. As much fun for me as it was to know I was allowed to hide next to her, my greatest feeling of acceptance came when she would gather everyone who was 'safe' and form a chain. Hand in hand, they were the connection that shortened your trip to the pole. I would run to her at the end of the line and be completely out of breath grasping her hand at the end of the human chain.

Safe. No one could touch me. I would not be the dreaded 'it' as long as I held her hand.

It was hard to imagine I was the elder.

It is hard to imagine that I am her killer.

I made good grades throughout my pre-college career. She made better grades. I played computer games and sat in the bleachers, but only when invited. She focused on sports and kept in shape.

I grew tall and lanky and goofy, she was happy to be over 5 foot tall. She was popular, and although I was never close to it, she never made me feel like I was anything but. She was a good person, and never minded my desire to feel accepted and hers was the only tolerance of my insatiable exaggerations trying to seem better at life than I was.

Under my mother's persistence, I began taking college courses my junior year. By the time she graduated high school, I was on my last semester of college classes. She took that summer off and I pushed through hoping to land a job and gain the influence of financial success. My plan worked, except she went away to study abroad and only had my words to see my moderate success. The ratio of my correspondence to hers was embarrassing, and her responses were just that; responses. She never would elaborate about her situation, and I was never clever enough to ask. I just rattled on about what I was doing and she gave a 'good job', in a hundred words or less.

The lengthier the time grew between her responses the more persistent I became. It was when she stopped writing for an entire semester that my stream of one-sided conversation led me to the idea of visiting her. Her lack of responses never allowed her to deflect my advances and I did not hear from her until I had already purchased a ticket to Liverpool.

She was cordial about the whole thing. She set up a cot in the front room of her flat, and made a spare key for me. She found guides of the city and things to do. She planned a visit for me that did not involve her, and I took it as a sign that there was a chance.

Somehow.

I thought the day we had planned together was the first day of the rest of my life.

And it was.

Samantha Atwater, dead at 22.

(II)

Robert Garin Carlyle, reborn at 24.

And I was.

It is the break of dawn and I have found myself doing pull-ups on a pole just outside of my metallic residence. Combined with my constant walking I have begun to form a new shape and am honestly pretty proud of myself. The more I see my name in the paper the less concerned I get. It seems the information, as detailed about my past and as far from the current truths it is, puts me at ease as far as what I need to find.

I need to connect any one of the deceased, Samantha included, to any of the other deceased. Or one of the three men disconnected to all the social networks they have painted them to be in. It seems no one from those businesses are stepping up just yet to say that the men do not work there. I, also, cannot prove they did not work there just yet. I am definitely confused as to how all the pieces are put together, but such random pieces give me hope that there is not just one puzzle. These writers try their best to make it seem like everything fits together so smoothly. Proof as to multiple puzzles, or just one really big puzzle, and I will consider myself a free man.

All of that or I am just a serial killer with no motive. I'll give them the fact that I am a killer, but that's the wrong adjective. And I have such a motive now that I do not know how I can be stopped.

I just need to figure out how to begin.

Flexing my biceps, I breathe in deep. I grab a shirt that lay next to the two other ones from the ground and put it on. I stack my newspaper clippings up on top of a small plastic crate that usually forms as my coffee table or dinner table, depending on the time of day, and use a rock for a paperweight.

I walk to the docks and take in the beauty. The gulls. The smells. The morning combustion of small talk and boats starting. If my hair weren't so dark I might be mistaken for a Californian surfer. It's in my eyes now, feel like I'm hiding behind hid it. And everything else that is around me.

I am headed away from the private docks and up the ports to find some warehouses, or somewhere I may be able to get info a little less conspicuously. Along the way are the courtesy nods addressing me as a person, in addition to the complete dismissals as a man on the street, but mostly just people doing what they do. I can hear the cranes working as I get closer to where the large freight containers are being unloaded. The sound of hundreds of men loading and unloaded, moving and relaying, talking and yelling, start to overrun the morning.

Their early morning work-ethic makes you feel like the sun is a lazy piece of shit that should have been on the scene at least an hour previous. I feel quite lethargic just walking into their sight. I watch for a little while trying to decipher who was who, not just who was giving orders, but who was the right person to approach. I looked for the meanest looking man I could find who was holding the most responsibility on his clipboard.

I walked up confidently to the man who wore the most frustration on his face. He looked up at me with eyes that meant 'go away'.

"I'm looking for work", I didn't bother with any accent aside from my own. He looked further away before he looked back down at his paperwork. I did not insult him by repeated my statement. I just waited.

He took a deep breath and drew out the moment a bit longer. He did not even begin to look up in my direction, "You're two hours too late."

"I can be here at any time." I meant it.

"The pay sucks." He finally looked up, "...and it's not as glamorous as you think it is." I responded to his mild humor with mild stoicism. He did not even get a courtesy smile out of me, I felt it would not help. He looked at my shoulders and my legs and turned his head with thought. The small shaking of his head seemed like I was bound to disappoint him, "5am tomorrow morning." I nodded my head slightly with acceptance and turned only to return again tomorrow early.

"You'll be headed to Dublin, son. Be prepared for a full day." He called to my back as I walked away.

I walked away.

Too easy I thought to myself. I played that perfectly and now I have just got to get on the boat and find someone. Anyone who I can ally myself to. I have to be patient, though. I could barely contain the excitement coming from my heart and my lungs about my early morning success. My blood rushed through my veins with the opportunity. I began to smile and instinctively looked upwards, moving more blood through to my thoughts as my chin rose with pride.

Then I caught sight of waves crashing against themselves in the distant waters. My head leveled, and the boil of blood eased. I shrugged my shoulders back bringing scapulae together with a deep breath and released it slowly, looking back upon my path. Still walking, I paused my mind.

Confidence and patience outweigh pride and excitement.

I came back along my usual path and picked up yesterday's paper that awaited me. I already had read it yesterday but saw no point in disrupting the symbiosis that was occurring every morning. I walked more slowly even than usual as I made my way over to one of the three coffee places I jumbled up each morning to keep as a regular at irregular times.

No sugar, no cream this morning, I just wanted to taste the grounds. Breakfast was to be two muffins, one blueberry and one plain. I took my goody bag nearer to where I stayed each night and found a bench overlooking the docks. My coffee was half gone by the time I arrived, and I put it directly underneath me to cool off even more while I ate at my pastries.

I was pushing myself to relax as though it were the last day of the last vacation I would ever take. I savored every second. Every passing breeze. Every bird's song and every wave upon the passing waters.

I was ready to go home.

I was ready to find what I was made of and test my sea legs. Stocking and carrying and loading was going to kill me, I knew that for certain. I do not believe my body is ready for that much activity tomorrow, but my mind is ready for the next step. It will be a happy balance, I can feel it. I do not believe I have ever been more certain about anything in my life.

Watching the boats today was new again. There would be no sails on the cargo ship I would board tomorrow, and I could not fathom how the wind would influence the ship at all. Possibly in gasoline usage, possibly in direction, I just don't know.

The rest of my day will be spent gathering my will and constitution. I must absorb quickly and stay mostly anonymous. I cannot even think of what I will do when they ask me my name, or any other official stats.

What's your name, son? Robert Garin Carlyle, sir. I'm wanted for murder, by the way. Oh… and my friends call me Rob.

(III)

Enthusiasm or excitement, or perhaps a little of both, but I am unable to put it at ease throughout the remainder of my day. My routine as of late had not been much. Today it felt even less than that. I felt unaccomplished and out of tune with the real world. The more down on myself I got about where I was and what I was doing, the stranger my position became.

I was an official fugitive. I had been framed for murder.

Murders.

Well, at least the circumstances of the murders were a frame-job.

And I was about to thrust myself into a semi-public position. But I have to have the change. I have to take the risk. There is something bigger than me at work here and I have to figure it out.

Of course, this could also be the first step in running from my problem...

Sleep would need to come, and soon. I was not exactly equipped with an alarm clock and, although it would not really ruin my situation, not showing up early tomorrow for day one would keep my situation right where it is.

I am definitely ready to move in some direction.

Sleep is turning out to be a difficult direction to turn altogether. Recently I had even found myself getting used to this traffic jam of a sleeping arrangement; still and uncomfortable. Sleep did come, however, just not in the form I anticipated.

Wanting so badly to fall asleep, I eagerly let it take me when it finally came. I knew at once that I was dreaming and was honestly a little excited that I could be in control. I walked out of my room as a child and into my parents' living room they have now. The combination of the two houses reassured me that I was dreaming. Again, I relished the fact that I was getting sleep and took full advantage of testing my memory in their living room.

No one was there, and I was alone to look at photographs or furniture or, really, anything I wanted. Mounted on a wall were my school pictures starting from grade school. Mom had them mounted similarly to my father's pictures which were next to them. Both circling around the frame like a clock going from 1st grade at the top around to the 12th grade. I always loved that the grade numbers were off by one as a clock would actually be. My 7th grade picture would always remind me of 6 o'clock sharp… or was it the other way around? I never knew. I still don't. I smiled and looked at the photos missing from my dad's frame. 2nd grade, better known to most as just 1 o'clock, had mom's handwriting on a little piece of construction paper that read *"cough cough, stayed home sick."*

I tested my memory during this dream and looked over at the other missing photo over in the 9 o'clock position. Dad would have been about 15 or 16 then in the 10th grade, and mom must have known him to be trouble, as this time she had scrawled *"tsk tsk, skipping school."*

I turn and walk through their living room towards the television. They were into the modern world enough to have purchased a flatscreen television, but I had to laugh at their big bulky entertainment center. There were even slots embedded in one area for CDs. The television was wide angle and the space for it was large, but square. The excess gap showing the age of the crafted wood brought me comfort.

I look at my feet. Bare. Displacing the carpet like shallow water. If I am going to make the most of this dream I should take it outside. By the front door I see my shoes and I walk to them. Sitting on the small wooden stool in the front hall I start to put the shoes on and am flooded with mom's voice telling me about how I needed to go sock-sock then shoe-shoe and none of that sock-shoe sock-shoe business. She always felt there needed to be balance even when dressing yourself.

Fortunately for me I was dreaming. I did not need any socks and I put my dream shoes on anyway. I sniffed slowly trying my hardest to gather in some of their scent before I left.

I exhaled and opened the front door and walked out pulling the door shut behind me. I did not feel it close. Turning back towards the door the house is gone and I whip back towards what should be the front yard.

I am in large greenhouse. I stand towards the center of what I can only imagine is an herb garden about 100 square foot.

The glass windows are perfectly clear, and every fourth pane is a plastic tarp that is rolled up allowing for outside air to blow through. The light breeze combines the fragrant bushes and it smells like I am inside an Italian pizza crust. I see an area of rosemary bushes and am drawn to it.

The spiky leaves are soft to the touch and I reach way down to hold a limb near the base. I pull my hands up gently letting the soft bristles run through the palms of my hands until I have touched every leaf on the branch. I bring my hands together in front of my face and inhale. On the hard-black plastic plant holder it is written 'A1'. I ponder for a moment and look around.

On the wall nearest me I see an 'F' and to my right I see another wall about 35 feet away. On it are the numbers 1 through 10 written about as big as the F was. I look back at the wall with the F and see that it is actually part of the other part of the coding around the room and with it are the rest of the first ten letters in the alphabet. I lean down and lift the rosemary bush.

Its many branches trying to tickle my face I allow for the fragrant herb to attack me with all its might. At A-1 I find a small gathering of rosemary bushes and put this one down with those. I note a door nearby and consider leaving, but instead look back at the section of the greenhouse I was in.

I see a basil plant. Full and beautiful with a thick trunk nearly an inch around. I pluck a leaf from the center of one of the branches and roll it in my hands. Cradling the broken foliage, I bring it to my nose and inhale the new scent my skin has taken on. The aroma is overpowering, and I almost lose sight of the fact that I am still in a dream. I refocus and look upon the plastic molding that holds the basil: C-4. The bright white writing perfectly formed upon the smooth black plastic gently begs me to take it home. It's not far and I can see a mess of basil plants in the area that could only be accused of being C-4.

I make the trip with the plant in hand and quickly browse the basil plants looking for an outcast. I find it. It is a small strawberry container which is the same green in color as the small strawberries it holds. I-9 is printed on both long sides of the rectangular planter. I look back at the door near A-1.

I lean down to lift the strawberries and pause. I can smell the basil clearly and behind it I can see cluster after cluster of what could only be cilantro or parsley. I left the strawberries there.

What a sensory game I could play with my memory in this dream. Smell, sight, movement… the strategy game of mapping the plants to the area in the greenhouse was even appealing to me, but the door at A-1 was far more appealing.

I-9 would have to wait for tomorrow night.

I slowly made my way to the door. I imagined I was about to be outside feeling that same breeze lofting aromas around in the greenhouse, but as I opened the door there was only darkness. I turned back towards the plants and only a brick wall stood to greet me.

My eyes adjusted, and darkness grew to dimness, but not much better. The only thing more striking than my loss of vision was my loss of smell. I bring my hands up hoping for basil or rosemary and I breathe in dust. The discomfort immediately brings about coughing and a voice calls out, "Calm down yer coughin' and bring me another slab."

I see a long flat dolly nearby and granite slabs leaned against walls everywhere. The voice belonged to a man near a tool bench. There was a piece of granite on his workspace with four nearly-perfect edges. The last edge, dripping with wetness from his tile cutter, was about to be complete.

I clapped my hands together getting as much dust off of them as I could. I found a large piece of granite and loaded it onto the dolly. As he finished off the piece he was working on I approached.

"Not that one, that's too small and not even the right color." I looked at the piece and honestly could not tell it from any of the other strangely shaped two-inch this rocks piled up around this place. "Over there" he nodded with his chin, "I-9."

Sure enough there were numbers and letters along the walls, only here they went on forever and the writing was not so clear as it was in the greenhouse. I went to I-9 as defiantly as I could, hunting all-the-while for A-1 and a doorway.

At the correct marker for a piece he wanted I began to lift a side of a slab and work it onto the dolly. It was large, and quite heavy. Its thinness was deceiving as I could tell it was sturdy, but I was certain that if it fell down flat it would crack. I used the top of my foot as a fulcrum guiding one side of the granite onto the dolly and, with the clever reminder of this being a dream, got the other side up without issue. Wheeling the dolly back to the tile maker I saw the door just beyond him. He saw me see the door, "You can get after we finish, I need two more large pieces to finish off today's work." He flipped a switch and the noise echoed off the shallow ceiling. I cringed as though the sound were too bright of a light to look at.

I made my way back to load the granite. I worked two more large slabs on the dolly and worked with the new weight on the dolly to get it moving. It was much slower, but I was ready to leave this place. I finally made it to the craftsman who, without ever shutting off his saw, nodded with disappointment towards the door. I took the permission and left.

As I reached for the doorknob I hesitated, wishing for a moment that I could re-enter the greenhouse, or find a better chore here, or, even better, just sleep and stop this dreaming nonsense.

Turning the handle, I realized there was no turning it back. Everything went dark again and, where smell had been vacant from this place, foul rotting odor filled my nostrils. At first, I was impressed with the power of a dream, but the reality of this being a dream disappeared as the dimmest of lights revealed a horror.

Bodies.

Dead.

Everywhere.

There were hundreds, thousands or more, dead decaying bodies overlapping and covering every piece of floor I could see. Through the dim light I could not make out any walls, but stairs going up and down endlessly were everywhere.

And all of them littered with the dead.

I wanted so badly to feel again the stinging of the tile saw's screech in my ears. I wished for the sweet sweet aroma of lavender. I longed for the warmth of my parent's house. I needed to awaken.

I looked around this nightmare and knew two things: This indeed was a dream and if I found a way out of this room of death the next room was not likely to be any better.

I closed my eyes and waited trying not to inhale the stench. I held my breath.

Finally, I awoke. I opened my eyes just long enough to see that I was in the real world. I brought a hand up over my eyes and smelled the clean familiar air. I stretched and rose to greet the new day.

It was dark outside, and I did not plan on bringing much, if anything, with me. As I walked out of my room with no door I dared not look back. I just hoped that it was going to be waiting for me when I returned.

(IV)

Walking onto the docks, I find it's a quiet morning. I only hear the water and my footsteps falling heavy upon the solid wood beneath me. It is still dark outside, and I am thankful that I have awoken so early. The path before me is easily navigated and I close my eyes. The added darkness is not too inhibiting as it was already dark, and this is a path I have walked many times.

I move my thoughts through my dream again. This time the thoughts of my parents' living room is not so pleasant as I know the final result. Their front yard replaced by a greenhouse. The aroma of nature and purity replaced by dust and darkness. Hard work replaced by death. Each door I chose to walk through, and each door closed behind me.

As real as it was, it was just a dream.

I open my eyes and I see the harbor ahead. Such large ships ready to be unloaded and loaded again, readied for shipment. Only one man stands at the docks walking briskly away from the ships towards the small office just inside the harbor. He spies me and slows his step bringing his clipboard down to one side.

"I thought I would beat you here" and I regret my attempt at camaraderie as soon as the words pass my lips. The expression on his face did not change for a moment, but I could easily read his thoughts expressing complete doubt in that ability.

"I'm glad yer here, son. I lost two good men yesterday." He scratched his forehead and smirked at his own statement, "It's not what you think." Turning head first in the other direction I am beckoned to follow, "I will need you to fulfill the duties of both of them today, y'hear?" His voice a little louder now that he is facing away from me. He comes to a halt, turns and looks at me. He finally smiles, "I expect you to fail that need."

I accept that I am likely unable to fulfill the duties of two men. Even if they each only had half a day's work between the two of them, that's a full day more than me. And there are two of them.

Were.

For whatever reason.

The twenty or so minutes I have with just the supervisor is valuable. It is greater information than I will receive for the remainder of my day.

I am essentially a grunt, which sounds great to me and works out perfectly. I am treated as though I am incapable of doing anything, and the constant micromanaging gives me the ability to complete tasks I would normally not understand at all. I can see veterans getting frustrated with the "guidance" and I mimic their frustration... slightly, hoping to look more like the Pope than Prior Dom Galliard.

Throughout my morning I am easily one of those marked as slower than the rest, but I am never given grief for incomplete tasks as there have been none. I hope that is all that ultimately matters, and I know I will grow in skill and speed. With cranes and trucks and wenches, I actually have not lifted too much, but I am definitely feeling the brunt of a solid morning's movement.

I have done more activity in the past four weeks than likely my entire life, but today tops off my days as the most brutal I have ever faced. And we have only loaded the ship to prepare for voyage to Dublin. My day is not even half over from what I can assess.

I am happy to have been chosen among those who will board and make the voyage over to unload what we've put on this morning. There are fewer than half of us that started, and honestly it seems as though some who were not chosen are a bit hurt by it. Of course, you can see some contentment by a few others as well.

The scene on board is not quite what I expect. I pictured magic and brotherhood like the pirate stories I never heard but always imagined as a kid. I walked along the main deck, and no one paid any attention. It seemed this was as much personal time as anything and I thought I would use it to observe. What I observed mainly was that I was the rookie here.

But my curiosity of the sea outweighed my desire to blend in. The men I was so busy busting my ass with this morning were either resting or starting to eat the lunch they had brought with them. I did not have the foresight to bring a lunch.

The main deck did not test my legs the way I imagined. It felt solid and like the ground I was used to throughout my entire life leading up to this moment. I hated to feel disappointment, but I believe I did. What I did not feel, however, was that this was a true test of my "sea legs". This vessel was too big. Too heavy. And we were not yet out into the Irish Sea.

I stayed out on the front of the deck for as long as an hour. I did not leave until I could not see the shores for either side of the boat. The entire voyage was damn near 9 hours total. The men gathered in a small room that forced talk along the same lines. Many of them knew each other. Those were the ones it was easy to keep at bay from too personal of questions. The most difficult of questions was brought about the most often and was a query to my name.

Mark Twain said, 'If you tell the truth you don't have to remember anything.' I took this to heart as much as possible.

"Robert" I replied as quickly and honestly as I could each and every time it was asked. I was thankful for the times my last name was not asked, which for this trip, was every time. These men were not too curious, and I believed that beyond asking for my name, if they remembered it past my two-syllable statement of a response, they hardly listened to a word I said.

As hungry as I was, I was pleased to find no one asked why I did not bring a lunch, nor if I wanted part of theirs. I longed for a bite to eat but could get by hoping for a moment in Dublin that I could steal away and find a bite. I rubbed the inside of my right thigh feeling the thick envelope of cash under my jeans.

Many of the men fell asleep in the tight quarters and I found a quiet moment to head back out onto the deck. I was not sleepy, hungry for certain, but not sleepy. I stayed near the railing of the front of the ship until the edges of the water showed signs of land.

The salt in the air smelled like déjà vu.

The water was beautiful. The waves felt like my thoughts and kept my mind occupied for every moment that I stood there.

I was at home. It did not matter the vessel that I stood upon, I was at home.

(V)

Although I was still naturally scared of getting a sunburn, I stayed on the bough of that deck for far longer than any stint I may have had at the beach.

Ever.

The nape of my neck would definitely be hurting tonight, and I was afraid of the burnt thin skin on my nose, but being away from the earth and into the salty escape of the sea was a first for me. I found a second wind, despite my lack of dinner on the ship, and found myself keeping up with some of the veterans on the decks of Dublin.

As we entered I watched ships and sails move aside from our large vessel. The thin canals entering Dublin seemed like such a maze to me. From the first sight of the coastline the Irish Sea failed to feel as flat as it had for nearly 4 hours.

Like a profile view of corduroy, the docks of Ireland's coast went on forever. I was amazed just knowing that this captain must know exactly which seem within the fabric we would be leading into. From such a distance it felt as though he were guiding a seaworthy skyscraper into a keyhole from 19 miles away at 35 knots.

I had confidence in him.

Cranes replaced the thousands of men I expected to see waiting for us. There were a couple crew members dressed in bright orange awaiting with thick ropes where we were docking. I wondered who from this boat oversaw catching the ropes or throwing one back.

Or calling to the men.

...or telling the captain we were here.

As the multi-ton vessel eased into settlement and found its resting spot within the shallower waters of Dublin the men from the quarters entered the deck and made their way to dock for the afternoon.

Cranes swung towards the back of the ship and I felt that's where I needed to go. I hustled past the surprisingly few persons it took to tie the ship up and joined the bulk of our crew as they aligned the crane operators to our cargo.

Crate by crate the ship rose slightly in the water. It was more of an interesting thought to me than an overwhelming feeling. The subtlety of this ship gaining buoyancy as it lost weight was perplexing to the mind, but never enough of a jolt to awaken the easiest of sleepers.

Here I felt rather useless as nothing more than a guide to a crane operator who had done this countless times. His eyes from afar had to be better than my own up-close just from his experience alone.

He was too far away for me to even know what color his hardhat was, yet he could pinpoint the alignment of what seemed to me as a two-foot long string of iron Velcro.

Unloading did not take long. The crane operators here in Dublin seemed to outrank those of Liverpool. Both in skill and in numbers.

I came to a point where I could find virtually nothing to do. Normally this would mark a great proud moment for me, but here I felt I was missing out. That I was the lazy mark on the ship. That I was not clever enough to find a task and complete it. Here I was incapable of leading by example and I never had had that urge before.

Just at what I felt was my most lethargic moment the captain of the ship approached from behind me. My mind was startled but somehow my reaction showed no signs.

"Great job today. For a rookie to not quit and go sit below deck for the ride and forgo his pay in order to keep from working longer and JUST GET HOME is great. It'll be about an hour before they begin to reload and the crews on deck here don't need ya to help them. In fact, just stay out of their way. It's what you do in Ireland."

A slight nod from me acknowledging the praise and the advice.

"Been to Ireland before?" he asked, and I responded with an even slighter shake of my head. "Well go check it out. You've got the better part of an hour. Get whatever you want, just don't bring any of it back on the ship. Follow me?"

"Yessir." I reply, and he walks to the other members of the crew who were standing and watching just as I had been. I feel better about not finding anything to help out with. I turn towards the docks and do not see which side to exit from as there are docks on both sides of the ship like a piece of old dried rice stuck between the prongs of a fork. I head starboard and walk down the ramp leaned carelessly against the ship. Walking the ramp takes more out of me and my balance than did the entire trip collectively. I wonder if this is the plank and I have been found guilty of mutiny. I smile as I catch my balance again and try to keep from flailing my arms around.

If I were to fall it would only be about a 15-foot drop to the deck below.

But I do not fall, and I only wave my arms like a tool once before gaining my footing on the dock.

Suddenly the earth feels solid. I take a couple steps and have to regain composure as I did not realize the extent my equilibrium had been at play. Each step is a chore and it feels like I have been on a trampoline jumping for hours with my friends and each of us has hopped off and are trying to jump on solid ground again.

As my gait corrects my hunger rises. I am suddenly so hungry I worry that the thought of eating will put me in a food coma.

Finding food was not difficult. I went the opposite direction of a large crowd of men talking eagerly and seemingly refreshed. Their accents seemed fake to me and I had to convince myself of how true accents really are. It is a realization I have often, but now that I have finally become used to the English accent, and the even stranger dialects from Liverpool, a new accent floods curiosity into my mind. The Irish make me feel as though my favorite character from a book has come alive and introduced themselves with a name, although spelled the same as I had read over and over, pronounced unlike anything like I would have ever guess. Glancing quickly around for where those men ate their lunch I am humored internally at the thought of some clever writer purposely putting normal words into the mouths of their characters knowing full well the pronunciation would be different with each reader.

I was hoping to find tacos and dreading that I would only find falafel. I did find fish and chips and felt a grand desire to go heavy on the coleslaw option. As I ate I felt I had made the right decision.

I walked quickly along the docks of Dublin, one, to not feel groggy after quite a bit of fried foods, and two, to see as much of Dublin as I could in one hour.

According to the late afternoon sun I was heading Northwest. I was out of the shipping district much quicker than I anticipated and was happy to look to my right and see sails drifting along the endless horizon. I walked out to see and checked my watch. Failing to have looked at my watch when I left I had to do some quick life calculations to figure how long I had walked and how long it took me to eat. I presumed I had about 20 minutes more of leisure.

I saw it immediately. The Pearson 424 docked happily less than a mile from where I had just finished off my dinner. I approached without fear. I knew this was the stolen sailboat and I felt I was a part of it. I glanced quickly around for signs of onlookers, but nobody seemed to be paying much attention to me at all. I boarded the vessel.

Unlike the cargo ship I spent the last 6 hours with, these were not the sturdy footings I was used to. Although I did not waiver, I definitely had to concentrate on my legs.

This is what I had been waiting for.

I wanted to run and test myself immediately. I grew fond of my new enthusiasm and felt proud of being a man for the first time in my life. What would normally have struck me as rude curiosity, my confidence was like a fire in my chest. I walked with my hand along the railing and overlooked the brushing sea against the side of the boat. If I had felt at home before, I had just hung the family portraits on the wall.

Walking this ship and feeling its potential below me was the closest to ownership of anything I had ever felt. I was ready to defend it with my life. Against theft, against time, and against the ocean itself.

I made one lap around the Pearson and looked down at my watch. I would be early, hopefully, but I would take my newfound pride back to work.

I took one last look back at my boat as I left the docks and took a deep breath. Maybe it was not my possession after all, but it sure was inspiring.

PRAYER AT MAST

The hopes, the wishes and the confidence from those living at sea.

(I)

"How's your boat?" Bradly asked as Curtis walked into the small diner. Curtis said nothing, not even grimacing at his large friend and his awkward attempts at humor through mental discomfort. Bradly smiled towards his criminal friend, but more so about himself. It was early, about 5:45, and the diner was nearly half full. Bradly had already been to work, having arrived around 5 that morning, and did enough to set everyone up for the day and justify having a management position. He likely would not return until around 9 or 10 this morning if he went in at all. Coffee was set down next to Curtis. He reached for all the sugar packets in the little rectangular container set on the table against the carpeted wall. Bradly pushed the half-filled creamer over to Curtis. Curtis shot him a glare as though Bradly offered him cream every time they had coffee together. And he did.

"No cream, huh?" Curtis looked down at his dark black brew and kept stirring. "You still put enough sugar in your fucking coffee to revive a family of diabetics." Curtis looked up at Bradly through his brow, still yet to have spoken since he awoke. "Your goal of trying to look like a coffee purist and convince other purists that you drink your coffee black is not going to work." Curtis raised his head up with peaked interest in his friend's upcoming point. "You may not be tainting the color of your brew but if you don't stop stirring and pull that goddamned spoon out of there you're just giving it away that you can't handle your coffee black like a real man should."

Curtis stopped stirring and slowly pulled the spoon from his cup. His friend of so many years had him pegged. He did avoid creamer just to keep his coffee "black". Strangely enough for a man who kept out of everyone else's business, he always assumed he was being watched. And the perception he wanted to present to all the eyes that were on him was one of a pure black coffee drinker.

But no one was watching him. Only himself. And Bradly, of course, would always be watching just to point out the awkwardness Curtis brought upon himself trying to not look awkward.

"When are ya taking off in that boat?" Bradly got to the point. "Gibraltar's pretty far to go by yourself…"

Curtis sipped his coffee and was trying to find words formed, but it was still too early for words. He wished he could just speak to his talkative friend thought to thought, but even his thoughts were not yet clear enough. He looked back down at the table and picked the spoon back up to finish stirring all the sugar not yet saturated into his 'candied' coffee.

Bradly leaned in with both elbows on the table, it was the least amount of room he could overtake around the table they were sitting. "Do you need supplies, money, passports… company?" Curtis' mind suddenly cleared up as he realized where his friend was going with the conversation. Leave it to Brad to get to the point as quickly as possible. Curtis leaned back and took a deep breath inviting Bradly to do the same. He blinked heavily, leaned his head forward to rub one eye, and inhaled deeply once more leaning back again.

"It really is supposed to only be me. I think part of it is their need for secrecy and the other part is, and I really got this impression with all the technical questions he was asking, but I believe they want to know if I can do something like this solo."

"Who is he?" Bradly quipped.

"Honestly don't have any clue." Bradly squinted at the comment and Curtis continued before he could ask all the obvious questions. Curtis' mind was clearing out its morning haze, "I never actually met him, never actually spoke to him, to tell the truth. Everything was through correspondence and I didn't even use the same method each time."

"Each time?"

"Three times actually." He pondered his coffee and took a big drink, "Once was an inquiry about if I was capable of everything. Very general information about my capabilities. It actually seemed they were asking questions very pointedly and, well in hindsight, very specific about where I would be going and if I could do it. The next time I heard from them it was a different person, but just like the first time they found me early in the morning while I was alone having my coffee. This time they brought money. It was only enough to get me to Liverpool and to buy me dinner but was still sufficient to get me on the hook. Before I left I was presented with another amount of cash. This time it was with information about the route to take and delivery the Pearson. The information included more than enough money to get me to the delivery spot."

"Enough to get you back home?"

"No."

"Do you trust them?"

"No."

"I guess that's smart. You gonna take enough to get you back?"

"Man, I don't really have it. But I'm not sweating it too much. If they don't give me the money I can manage. I'll find a crew or, shit, steal a boat." Curtis started to laugh at his conclusion when Bradly showed no signs of a smile.

"If they don't give you the money to get back, they may remove all capabilities of you getting back, if you catch my drift?" Curtis knew that if they did not pay him that it likely meant they were intending to have just used him as a means of obtaining the boat. Then they would have the boat and no need for him. He had considered that option but did not waste any moments worrying about it.

61

"Yeah, there's always that."

They sat quietly for nearly fifteen minutes. Curtis finished his coffee right away and pondered if he was going to refill it. He always did, but he also always considered it. Bradly sat more quietly than Curtis had ever seen him. He was more interested in this excursion than he ever had been before. Mostly he asked questions after a trip. It was curious that he was so intrigued about his trip before he left.

"I'm leaving tonight." Curtis finally broke the silence.

Bradly's acknowledgment was a quiet one and the silence again swallowed up their conversation. Curtis got a fresh cup of coffee and stirred in more sugar. The thought of a long solo trip was comforting to him and the anxiety of relaxation was always an interesting feeling for him. The anticipation of comfort both soothed and made for slightly more discomfort just with the acknowledgment of it. Like when you're cold, so you try to imagine yourself walking on a warm beach... but you're actually soaked in freezing rain. Curtis always tried to imagine a worse condition instead of a better one so that the current condition seemed a bit better. He felt it was his natural, optimistic approach to life. However, the thought of two days alone on a boat was such a comfortable thought that any other situation seemed dreadful to him. He moved uncomfortably in his seat as Bradly was unwavering in his stoicism.

"I suspect that *when* they pay you you'll want to stay and do some sight-seeing... so I'll see you again in a couple weeks?"

Curtis nodded with small rapid movements, bit his bottom lip before taking a big swig of sweetened black coffee. He rose.

"I'll see you in a couple weeks man. Thanks for everything." He dropped a couple dollars on the table and left. Bradly reached out and gripped the dollars shoving them unfolded into a front pocket. Leaning in the opposite direction in his chair he fished out a cell phone from his opposing front pocket. As Curtis left the small diner Bradly sent a quick text.

Leaving tonight. He won't disappoint.

(II)

The trip would take eight to twelve days by his best calculations. And that was just to get to the South of Spain. He did not have the faintest clue to the wind conditions through the Bay of Biscay. He barely knew the ways of the Celtic Sea as he rarely ventured too far from the sight of the UK shore. But he had crossed over to France before. And he most definitely had been to Amsterdam a time or three.

Egypt seemed so far away for a simple sailboat. If anyone were to make it with anything beyond luck, it would be Curtis. He was mentally prepared. Excited even. He looked forward to finding new features of the water to challenge him. His endurance he knew would be no problem. Days out at sea brought him closer to complete, even if those that knew him could argue that there would always be pieces missing from the puzzle that was he. It wasn't the boat he felt he knew so well, but the water and the wind. The elements that he had no control over were the voices he heard telling him about the way things were. The boat was just the tangible that he could manipulate to the best of the opportunities brought to him from the natural. Estimates for a sailboat moving along the ocean are right about 6-9 nautical miles per hour. Which for land-lovers equates to about 7-10 miles per hour. Curtis knew he had somewhere between 1700 and 2000 miles to travel just getting to Gibraltar. Unlike a road-trip, however, there was not a marked road to follow or a set speed limit. In fact, Curtis was completely allowed to go as fast as he possibly could. Hell, he even had an engine he could use if there were no natural elements pushing him the right direction.

He fully expected the current to be mostly against him. The rushing waters from the Mediterranean Sea entered the Atlantic and took a swift turn to the right, or Northward. He would be relying mostly on the wind to carry him through the Celtic Sea past the Bay of Biscay to the Atlantic Ocean proper before he might catch some helpful Southbound current off the coast of Portugal and back into Spain again near the Strait of Gibraltar. That super salty Mediterranean water was much heavier than the salt water of the Atlantic, so Curtis was hoping to pick up speed around Portugal as the Northbound waters would be deep under the surface and likely to displace the cooler Atlantic waters towards his midpoint entering the great Mediterranean. He would have to wait to pass two-thirds of the first half of his trip to see his theory in action.

The waters leaving the Irish Sea were fairly crowded with other ships, and as he was more inclined to the ways of the wind than the engine, he would have to keep watch of his direction until at least he reached the bigger waters of the Celtic Sea. The wind nearer lands were more predictable and steadier and made easy traversing for the skilled sailor. At night he was thankful for the big lights each cargo ship had. A couple times he allowed himself to cat nap. He trusted the distant lights of other ships and the lights of his own P424 and settled down in the cabin letting the wind carry him slowly South. He was comfortable with the thought that any boat large enough to ruin his ship, and too large to navigate around him, had the unfortunate expense of a loud obnoxious engine to wake him from his light sleep in time to get to the deck and steer clear.

For all his lengthy trips taking multiple nights with no one on deck to help him keep an eye out, he had never really had too close of a call. He was the one that was leaving his boat's course to the wind and most other sailors had crews to keep an eye out. Besides, he was over confident in anything he did already, what more was traveling blind in the vast open waters? With this much skill he needed some way to push his limits.

Overall, he accumulated about 4 hours of total sleep for the nearly 30-hour period it took to arrive at St. Mary's, the little holiday group of Isles a long ferry ride Southwest from the UK. He made his way around towards the south of the island groupings by way of the UK side and found a quiet place to dock. It was here that he finally able to find some solid sleep and let his guard down, as little as he pretended it was actually there. Sleep came quickly for the tired thief. From the lack of good sleep over a period longer than a day and the easy tides rocking the stolen sailboat quietly against a dock that didn't have the population on shore to care about who was there, just that someone was and would spend some money in the town so far away from the motherland.

Curtis was a day and a half into a journey which would change his life. He imagined how easy the sailing would be coming back. With the wind and the water in his favor, his biggest concern would be acquiring another boat after he sold this one. What he could not foresee was that he would not be sailing back from Egypt. What he could not foresee was that Egypt was not his final destination.

(III)

As tired as he was, he could not force himself to oversleep. He wanted to, but his excitement for this trip outweighed his need for sleep. In the night he was confident he had found the right dock and would rise to the deck of his boat to see the familiar little coffee shop he had visited whenever he sailed around England towards France from Ireland. The people of Tolman Café did not recognize him, but he was as familiar with their deck and their service and their coffee as he was with all of the outlying places he visited on his journeys.

He took a bath by towel with the cold water coming from the faucet of the restroom on board. He saw no big need in wasting perfectly good drinking water when he knew the next leg of the journey would leave him 3-5 days out at sea without docking. But he also did not want to be a complete slouch walking into a respectable business that would never allow his coffee cup to run dry.

He dressed himself and walked the quick flight of stairs to the deck of the Pearson. He had set himself up exactly where he had thought he had been in the dark of night. Very few lights in this small town to help a lone sailor. The tourists did not venture this way via this dock and the bright lights and welcoming signs were better positioned where the ferries coming from Great Britain arrived. He was hoping to just walk off the boat and up to the Tolman Café with minimal exposure. Which is exactly what he had set himself up to do.

He entered with a small group of tourists and their hustle and noise drew most of the attention from the small staff on duty for the morning. One bright young barista took notice of him and with a slight head raise acknowledged he was not with the group ahead of him. He raised the first finger of his left hand indicating it was just him and lifted a menu from the now unoccupied hostess stand to his right. The barista nodded understanding to all and motioned towards the deck and towards the bar for him to seat himself.

Curtis instead made his way to the more secluded deck. Here he could see the small bay, his boat, and avoid the conversation he knew would be had at the bar. He imagined having the opportunity of chatting her up on his trip back. He wondered if she would remember him a few weeks from now and played out a scenario where she welcomed him back. As the server present was occupied with answering questions about the menu and St. Mary's, the Isles of Scilly and Tolman Point, the barista made her way out to greet him.

Her long wavy brown hair seemed as if it had almost dried from her preparations for work today. She wore glasses that had little to no obvious prescription in them and Curtis marveled at the detail with which she accessorized, yet still seemed to have been running a little late for work. However, the look was a good one on her for him, and he so desperately wanted to be in a holiday position where he could give her more than just his order.

"Coffee and a coffee cake, please" he ordered after her inquiry. She noted they had a few types of coffee cake and asked if he would like for her to list them for him. "No thank you, I'll just have the one you're most fond of." As she reached for the menu to take it back he moved his hand towards the menu and wished he would have found the back of her hand instead of the laminate of the menu. "I'll hold onto that if you don't mind, I think I'm just getting started." His smile was met with hers and he loved the quiet understandings of her.

Perhaps it was too early for her, or perhaps she was just used to sailors not wanting to speak much, but he adored her for it.

Perhaps he was just alone at sea and she was close to him. He knew this probability but still embraced it. Her attention to him was nothing more than her mastering of her trade. She knew people like he knew a ship. Her liking to him was comparable to him having a ship he knew well, one that spoke to him easily, responded well and was easy to handle. Did he love that ship? Absolutely. But only because it got him closer to the sea. He was certain his ability to speak to her with more than the use of words gave him a slight advantage to others in her eyes, but not because of him.

He liked her more because he felt he knew her and that she loved what she was doing. He liked her more because he thought she was like him in that way. He liked her more because he knew what to expect as long as he sat on this deck and ordered more coffee.

The sea wasn't a place where he knew what would happen, but rather a place where he knew exactly what to do. The sea had no voice. The sea gave no warning. The sea was a difficult customer who you at first dreaded because you didn't understand how they had made it this far in life. As you get to know the sea you realize how powerful it is and how peaceful it wants to be. All these elements struggling from one place to another desperate to get there pushing and shoving to get there first paying no mind to those around it. Sailors trying to master a beast that can have no master. A beast that simply wants to lay waste and settle down. A monster of sorts that is only being pestered by the wind and the earth and the moon and life. It has been a constant mover, never ceasing and always the bane of others' existence. He knew the sea was restless and he loved it for that. Just as much as it didn't want to go out of its way to please anyone, it didn't really want to hurt anyone. It was too big to see the folly it could bring to any one creature, from the sea or from the earth.

And Curtis knew this. He knew he could never "master" the sea, only it's meaning. He never felt like he deserved more from the waters than he got and he knew if he didn't want to deal with the

Leslie Wootton

sea, he didn't have to go. Like the brunette bartender taking care of customer after customer, taking it all in, dealing with the upset ones, permitting the difficult ones, admiring the easy ones, but overall just loving her job and perfecting her art. She knew that even if she was the best service person on the planet it would not change the guests that sat at her bar, only the way she dealt with them.

Curtis knew how to deal with the sea.

He would sit at Tolman's for the next 3 hours picking at lunch and sipping on his coffee. He didn't contemplate his route, only the journey, for he knew it was the sea that would direct him. To make time he would sail a strong wind, but it would rarely be going in exactly the direction he needed to go. Currently due South, he would settle for anything with south in the description and make it work. He hoped to make good time getting towards Spain and Portugal. He hoped that the sea would not be still. He hoped the wind would be strong at his back.

He would get what he had hoped for.

VICE CAPTAIN

Stepping in to take control when it is lost.

(I)

I had been working non-stop. Every day. And on the long trips I didn't mind staying overnight, even if it meant sleeping in a cargo net on the boat. He offered a check, I needed only cash. He had asked for more info twice, I never provided it, the subject has been dropped.

As fortunate as I am that he has not pried into my info, it heightens my awareness to the situation. There has always been an excess of paperwork in a business system and I've always felt the system provided you a number. And you became that number.

But I was fine with that. Comfortable with that. I knew what it meant. Now he hands me cash, admittedly less than what would be coming in check form, but nonetheless it is cash in hand. I'm certain I'm not the only one and this isn't the first time, but I am too detail oriented to configure how he justifies it. Again, it's fine with me, I just do not see how he is ok with it.

I didn't know his name, I didn't feel it was really a secret, but everyone just called him Swansea. A few times I had overheard him called "Copper" and I made the wrong assumption it was because he was the boss, the overseer, the enforcer. But it turns out it was a regional thing and the entire city of Swansea was once known for its copper mining. Swansea was a giant peninsula itself protruding from Wales and surrounded by the sea. It would be hard to have grown up in Swansea and not be surrounded by the sea like the city you lived in.

Leaving for the day Swansea poised himself so that I knew he needed to speak to me. Always on the sly this guy, he never broadcast that he was doing anything other than observing. No objectives it would seem. Of course, looks were completely deceiving.

I approached with my usual confidence and conformation, ready to hear anything he had to tell me. As I approached he turned about 3 steps away from me and walked slowly away. Always in charge, that guy, he knew how to work body language to his advantage. I admired him for it. Subtle power in his every move. Not feeling shunned, more admiration of his course, I followed quietly knowing he would speak when he arrived where he wanted and when he was ready. I, of course, had to be ready the entire time as it was only he that had the leisure to prepare himself.

"You're still a fledgling, but you're definitely not a Jonah. The entire crew would attest to that no doubt." His strong pregnant pause seemed to have been a little more than he had expected. Perhaps he wasn't looking to give me any compliment at all and found what he would consider weakness in the statement.

"You've built a strong crew sir, that knows what you expect, and that is easy to learn from if you're paying attention and given a chance." It was a return compliment with a bit of self-lifting and he knew it. The tone was business awkward, as though someone decided jeans on a Wednesday was ok and the boss did it on the same day. Wasn't quite casual, just in the midst of the wrong company. And both parties knew it and were ok with it. Ultimately it meant for both of us to get to the point and that was why I saw us getting along. I was no longer in a position to small talk with anyone and felt more comfortable divulging details, possibly incriminating details, if it was to reach a means with someone that wasn't looking to expose anything but their own course of action.

"We are headed out earlier than usual tomorrow morning. Some guys think they have the day off, and they will for the next week, but you'll be joining the core of the crew and some new guys." I nodded my head. He assumed I would be on the trip. He assumed correct. "I need you to step up even more and ensure the success of any new crew members. My original crew doesn't take too kindly to train so many new guys, but they must be there." I caught on to everything he was getting at. He wanted me to be the bridge between the new and the old.

I had successfully gone under the radar and joined the crew in a short period of time. Mainly because there was only one greenhorn, me, and I needed to be here. From then on, there would be more than one, apparently, and I couldn't determine the factor that had made Swansea think they'd be useful on the trip.

"Aye sir. I'll make it right." He nodded as we seemed to do all too often. But we really did see eye to eye. Different routes of action, but always on the same page. He knew my weaknesses better than I did, but he wasn't going to tell me. He trusted I would find them all and that he could teach them to me one by one when the time was right.

I waited for further information as there was more he wanted to say. I could tell he was filtering the necessary info from the fluff and wanted to find as few words as possible to convey and end this conversation. I was fine with that.

"3am we leave. Be here on time to ensure of that. Loading has already begun and the ship will be at 3 quarters full up top. Precious cargo, Robert. And we must get it to Lisbon within 48 hours of sail."

"I'll get to the ship right away." I waited for his approval to leave my current post. Again, the nod of understanding.

What I heard from him was that some members of the crew were already loading the ship. There was never a good time to sleep on the ship, but sleeping now was the wrong time. Swansea didn't have to tell me that, he knew I knew. Also leaving before 3am with a 48 hour or less arrival meant we were shipping out before there were too many observers on deck and would arrive with the same veil of darkness in Lisbon. My mind raced to find what we were carrying. My mind also raced in the understanding that it was not important. At least not to me.

(II)

It wasn't so much that they were lazy. It wasn't so much that they weren't fit and ready for action. It wasn't even the fact that it was too obvious they took commands at their least amount of discipline to accomplish. It was that they saw a bigger picture and weren't worried about fitting in.

No matter how hard they tried to portray the opposite.

We had the ship loaded with tightly sealed cargo boxes before the requested time. The new help all wore clothes that had obviously been recently purchased and did not make too much of an effort to dirty them. The large heavy crates, bigger than mobile homes, were always latched down to keep the doors from flying open and creating hazards, but this time they were all locked shut. Not just a choice few with special cargo from well to do clients, all of them. If it weren't the standard for shipping companies to ship out at the lowest possible price and cram everything into any crate and not take the effort to lock it down, it would not have been noticeable.

The men never left the deck of the ship. They watched closely as each crate fit into the simple puzzle that was the deck. They seemed to cringe each time the crane lost the slightest bit of control and the wind moved two crates to crash loudly together. Those of us actually working knew that nothing could be inside those crates that would have been damaged by such a small encounter of such heavy objects. One would have to flip the cargo carriage on its side quite violently to stir up an issue with the contents.

Depending on the skill of whoever packed the carriage, of course.

The men I had now been working with for nearly a month did not talk that much in general. All work and just the necessary conversation to get the job done and check on each other's well-being from time to time. These were not the men who shopped for pleasure or strolled through parks. They worked and slept. And if there was dead weight in the form of help upon their ship, they had seen it before, and just picked up the slack knowing the dead weight would work itself out.

But I could see them taking ever so slight glances at the new help. Menacing glances. Spiteful glances. Observing glances. I had been instructed to be a liaison between the old and the new. Swansea knew there would be issues and wanted to quell the fire somehow. He knew that the lackadaisical nature of these guys, especially compared to his crew, would not go over so well. He had appointed me a nearly impossible task that I was certain he was aware of.

Complicated in that I was still not one of the boys even though I was no longer a scab on their daily routine. The freshly clothed ship jockeys paid no mind to commands or direction needed about the ship. None of them were close to considering a sit-down chat with me directing both sides on each other's needs and wishes to form a better union on the ship. I simply could only pick up the slack where they stopped short and ensure my part of the to-do list was properly cared for.

Swansea had been on board long before anyone took note of his being there. He had been on the radio with the crane operator and logged every stitch of detail necessary to record about the cargo before it had even been loaded. The detail book was far from public knowledge.

His cracked raspy underused voice came through the loud speaker on board and announced, "castoff at 15 til 0300." The idle engines immediately roared to action. Arguably already ready to ship off, the core crew checked and rechecked everything as the temp crew mingled helplessly as they had all morning, waiting to find the minimal in any requests of them.

All in all there were 7 members of the core crew and 4 of these intruders that Swansea brought to us to our dismay. Not counting the ship captain and those in the engine room, our crew normally consisted of 10 members for large shipments. This was not a large shipment, and the 7 core members were hardened and consistent. I, being the 8th if I was to be considered part of their side, was fully capable of supporting the 7 of them and handling this half-filled ship. The top half, actually.

Not needing the 4 of them made their presence even more of a distraction.

Swansea made his way down as the ship was released from the dock. He passed over the details on board he had trusted to his crew. Even knowing these guys refused to miss any detail, he refused even more. He was always determined to find an error and never had to say a word when he found one. His slight pause gave notice of the discrepancy, if ever there was one. It was corrected immediately and never repeated. At least not by the same man.

Today he was almost robotical in his inspection methods. Not known for a man who went on auto-pilot for anything, he droned about making his usual rounds. His thoughts were not with the crew's work. Doubtful it was due to a sudden spike in confidence over anything he hadn't done himself. Even if he had been the sole crew member of the morning, the inspection would continue as planned. His mind was heavy with thought. One may even judge that he had some quiet satisfaction that wore through the leathery salt-water hardened face of the aging sailor. He finished the inspection without notice of error or announcement that he was through.

One by one the crew made their way down to the cabin for their breakfast and coffee. Most would find early sleep while the waves nearer to Liverpool and the UK were much slighter than getting out into the Atlantic. Even a seasoned sailor found calmer rest in the stiller waters. The new crew members joined but sat apart as though it were a middle school cafeteria. As usual I was the last member of the crew off the deck and the last to arrive in the mess hall. I chose not to sit in the middle like some matchmaker trying to right a wrong. Instead I sat on the side, if you could call them sides, where the crew I knew was sitting. I positioned myself against the wall and kicked my heels up like I owned the place. This was no gesture of ownership or leadership, more of one representing the sailor who just wanted to take a nap. It was true. I had been awake for nearly 28 hours now and was really wanting to pass out. A hard-wooden chair and grown men milling around was just as good as a feather bed with Egyptian cotton sheets. Sleep came, but it did not come as quickly as I anticipated.

I listened to the sporadic comments coming from the men I had sat near for what seemed an entire new lifetime. I was bound to a boat that had no real legal system. No checks nor balances, and only one real judge. He was even believed to be able to overturn a sentence executed by the sea. The men talked of nothing and enjoyed that solace. Across the small room was a more quiet conversation that allowed for its members to take turns and participate. To follow what was being said and require some listening skills. I couldn't hear a word they said but their attitudes were very matter of fact. Details were being laid out. Past or present it was too difficult to tell exactly, but I guessed it was a little of both.

With their coveralls off, the men were suddenly not the skinny new guys they had seemed. They were skilled and athletic, obvious intelligence, but none of it was honed towards being on a cargo ship.

As the ship carried forward we settled in. I did my best observing but did not feel I would be gathering any additional information than I had already speculated on. I allowed my eyes to close. Just as everyone in the room disappeared from my sight, I no longer remained a participant in their world. As was the way on the ship. Let a sleeping man be.

(III)

I answered only in the manner in which I should have. I did not make up fairy tales about myself to portray me in any other light than what was true. I only intended on keeping that light dim and away from too many facts.

I was intent on doing a good job. The better I did the less notice was taken. The game was to keep myself in the mix of society, what little there was on the ship, and secrecy, what little inquiries came my way. I feared too long with the same men would bring up questions about my past. Who I was. Where I came from. How many people I had killed in the little Wavertree Park nestled within Liverpool… you know, small talk.

The memory was strong. Not haunting, simply present and vivid. Every day I had little more to dwell on. I had to keep reminding myself that the goal was not to blend in and start a new life. The achievement here was to set myself up quietly enough that I could get back to Liverpool and begin my own investigation. I still needed to see where those men were said to have worked. To talk to anyone in the offices that could verify that they worked there. Or prove they never did.

I refused to believe that these men were not connected as the paper would have you believe. I had left my newspapers back on the docks where I had built my temporary home. Those were my study guides. My motivation. My clues and my strategy. I did not feel safe bringing them on board. I felt the content was too specific and might draw a question. Any question.

"You seem pretty interested in those murders. Seems no one around town knew who those guys were anyway…" – would be the most confusing thing I could be approached by. In a world now where I am insisting on saying exactly the right thing at exactly the right time. In a world now where I could not give up any of my own information while gathering as much as I could find. In a world where a mistake on my part would give me up and finally bury any and all mistakes they could ever make.

Oh, how I wanted to make a friend and share my secret! To release myself of the burden I carried alone. To bounce my ideas on a wall of outside intelligence and see how the reflection of thought that came back my way really looked.

But it would not happen here. These men on this boat were not the men that wanted to be part of my investigation. In fact, if truth were to come out beyond this vessel, they would be irritated with just one reporter coming to speak to them about it. And there would be more than just one. This is why Swansea didn't mind supporting someone who didn't give his last name. Why he was ok with not knowing more. I was another hand on deck and that was all he needed as far as I could tell. No one here took mind of another's situation. No one here asked for handouts from the men they worked with day in and day out. No one here asked Swansea for a day's pay early or took notice if he did his arithmetic wrong calculating their wages.

He never got the pay wrong.

There were no cell phones or computers on this ship, only a radio. And everyone took turns avoiding it at all costs. There was no drama to be had. Most of the men were married and had children at home or had already left home. But you wouldn't know which those were. Their wives knew them as well as they could and were happy people knowing that their loyalty would always be there even if they were not. Drama was not to be had on this sailing vessel and if you could manage to start the conversation with anyone aboard, you would find quickly that no human quarrel was remembered. Only quarrel with the sea and loose cargo.

The four strangers did a poor job of blending in. They stuck out like an arctic glacier in the middle of a public swimming pool. The trouble was not so much trying to figure what their purpose was, rather in trying to conclude why Swansea allowed for such an undisciplined mass amongst his crew. Whatever was leading their conversation he knew about, and it was the first time he had allowed something beyond his men and his cargo and his discipline to exist within his command.

I stifled my curiosity to maintain my indifference. Whatever it was I was not going to be brought into it. I tried to justify my request from Swansea as a mediator to mean something more, but there was little to imply it was more than just a distracter to these men that didn't give a shit about four men that didn't give a shit. The corporate growth monger in me wanted the involvement. I wanted the opportunity to climb the ladder and work my way to the top. I wanted to feel each rung of information in my grip and to own the splinters under my skin as I climbed upwards and over anyone who dared to clutch the ladder before me. My desire to learn was out willed by the obvious notion that this ladder of success before me was leaning against the wrong wall.

This curiosity that fell before me on this ship, on this trip to Portugal, on this route through the Atlantic was nothing to me in my quest. I had to see it for what it was worth, which was nothing. If they had anything to do with me there would not be the obvious secrecy for which they worked. There would not be the tepidness in which I was to play mediator. There would be arrests. There would be accusations. There would be answers.

Finally.

Finally, I could either find those that had ripped me from my life and my ambition, or lack thereof, look them in the face and tear from them the reasons why they took Sam from me. Or be put away for her murder. Finally, I could solve all the riddles that are in front of me. Or be shut away without a chance to unravel anything.

Finally.

Finally, I would know if this journey was long or short. The short would mean that it was I who took the fall. The long path before me would have me finding those responsible, exposing them for what they are, and clearing my name. The short path appeals to the Robert that was before. Always determined but never acting upon that desire. Now I am nothing but action. My real determination would be to end it all but I cannot stop. I cannot allow myself to give in and take the blame for something someone somewhere wants to pin on me. I must continue this façade of a life living in the shadows of a cargo ship traveling from Liverpool to Ireland and back. And now down the western coast of Spain to Lisbon, Portugal. I found comfort in my sudden flurry of thought and began to doze.

Finally.

Finally, I would sleep with the burden of curiosity falling away. I would wake not more than a few hours after sleep found me. I would wake with a better view of what was before me. I would wake to see that I was still in charge of me and that none of these men, those of my recent past and those of my strange present, would be part of my future.

I would wake to be wrong about the effect those men would have on my future.

FIRST MATE

Ready to take control at the first opportune time.

(I)

Curtis could feel the Pearson 424 drift towards a more western direction. He knew the due south wind would not hold forever. He had slept longer than anticipated, however the easy movement of the wind did not alert him to any changes until now. He rose from the couch in the den of the cabin. The black television screen presented his own image to him and he sat back down on the couch to regain his bearing after awakening and standing so quickly. The change in direction was nothing startling, just a change. He was thankful it was not more easterly and pushing him closer towards the coast of Spain. Riding along the light coastal winds would not have been so bad, only slow. Amateur at best. He enjoyed the challenge of the bigger waters out towards the meat of the Atlantic.

He rose again from the couch sleepily and turned the coffee maker on that he had found in the cupboard the night before. It was a miracle he had found the coffee as the previous owner of the P424 did not have the common sense to keep it with the coffee maker. With the boat still on auto-pilot he made his way up to the deck to wait for the coffee to brew.

Still water sat below the ship's hull. He walked the bow and slid his hand down the rail taking him back to the rear of the vessel. Nostalgia from watching glorified Hollywood films would make an amateur feel that riding the nose of the bow of a ship was where it was at. The feeling of flying over the water. Seeing no structure under your feet and moving with the speed of the wind.

Curtis Scott was not interested in flying. He found comfort and solace in sailing. From the rear of any ship you felt like you were sailing. Because you were. It was real. It was tangible. And there was no feeling like sailing a ship as the only passenger. Having set your course and let the beauty of nature take over. To see the waves ahead and feel the movement of the boat underfoot. To sail.

It was the calmest he had ever witnessed the broad ocean. No land in site and nothing but cat paws toying at the top of the water's surface. He regretted blinking and having to miss even that slight moment of the life he had in front of him, even if each passing second looked like the last. Looking out at an endless ocean and the horizon boxing the compass, the idea of a flat earth boggled his mind. Each direction from his small pinpoint placement on the earth was downhill from him. Like an ant on top of a beach ball, there were no uphill movements on the surface. Smooth and in a downward direction, and it was only the same everywhere you went. Always on top of the world. Always an expression of momentum. Always above everything else.

With the sun warming his left side and the fresh scent of salted water tainting his every thought, he made his way back down to find the coffee he had forgotten he wanted so badly. He flipped the warmer off so that the coffee tasted fresh all day, even if the temperature wasn't the same. Cold fresh coffee tasted better than hot burnt coffee. He couldn't find any sugar in the cabin's kitchen, only sugar supplement. Curtis wasn't about putting artificial chemicals and enhanced food products into his body. At least not knowingly. He couldn't help but ignore his hypocrisy day in and day out, and refused to preach to others about their habits, but somewhere he thought he was right about all the processed food world, even if in fact he was pretty clueless. Just like everyone else.

He didn't buy into the conspiracy theory of anyone attempting to poison the world, he was convinced each product was there as means for some individual to find a way to make a dollar. Conspiracy sold newspapers. Facts moved us forward. The ocean kept him sane.

Hot unsweetened coffee filled up the oversized plastic tumbler he found in the half-sized dishwasher. He looked through the food stores and considered breakfast but concluded the tall coffee would be enough for a calm morning on the sea. The wind was starting to pick up with even more of a western focus now. The new sun and a strong reflection over the water brought a comfortable warmth with the wind. It reminded Curtis of driving in the winter with the windows down and the heater on full blast.

He knew better than to focus on the path ahead of him out on the water. It was everything that was behind you, out here, that pushed you forward. The wind and the waves are the past and the vessel is your present. You did not always have the opportunity to steer perfectly, only to react with the facts coming from the past, and the best opportunities presented with a well fashioned present. If your boat wasn't ready for a strong wind coming from behind you, then you were not going to make it where you were headed. Curtis' boat was equipped well enough, but that didn't make it easy.

He should have noticed the early morning light dimming so quickly. The large pillowy clouds rising in the East with the sun were growing more and more dense. And quickly too.

Pillows to billows in no time flat.

It didn't rock the boat, just yet, but the sails looked to take a deep inhalation of the early morning and they weren't about to exhale. Curtis turned over his left shoulder to evaluate. The clouds would still be considered white but were turning gray quickly and it wouldn't be long before they were of the blackest black. It was not the rapid changing weather that concerned him, but rather the slow rise of black smoke from the distant sea.

The scene looked as though the influx of bad weather was a major factor in whatever was on fire, but it wasn't likely. With so much water below, and a swarm of rain coming from above, the elements did not usually equal fire. In fact, if there was anyone affected by the fire, this storm would be good news. At least at the beginning when it tamed the flames. Not so much when the water rose up from below and struck down from above to make the sailor feel like an ember just trying to survive.

Aside from the brightness of the flame and the extended trail of smoke rising, there was very little to be seen with the naked eye. And it wasn't until the flickering flame went suddenly unnoticed that he could make out much more than fire plus smoke plus water. Something blocked the fire from his perspective, but the continuous smoke rising uninterrupted told him the flame still burned behind whatever was shielding his line of sight. The top of the pillar of smoke seemed to start bending towards him and dissipating quickly at its peak. The clouds behind began to darken and blot out the fire's plume from the top down. If he hadn't been watching the evolution of smoke and fire with usurping storm clouds behind it there could be an uncertain misconception of a tornado poised atop of a very thin stem.

But these clouds weren't spinning, they were rolling. The entire horizon was filling with the sight of a storm. From this distance it seemed minor, but he knew that noticeable movement that far away was not to be considered slow going.

The wind pushed the upwards momentum of the smoke suddenly to the right and less than a couple seconds later the distant flame presented itself again. Whatever was blocking the view had itself moved in the same direction. Obviously closer to him than the fire and smoke judging by the delayed reaction. For the fire to be visible at this distance it could not be small. He accepted something in his direct line of sight blocking the brightness of the flame backed by dark clouds, but it too must have been large. How could something so large be ahead of whatever wreckage was out in the open sea? He struggled at what it all meant until the flame was blocked out again.

Someone had hoisted a sail.

The adrenaline rush of escape suddenly flooded over Curtis. His eyes darted along the horizon searching for more information. With no obvious wind shifts in the growing darkness along the horizon, the sail kept a true direction towards his ship. Miles away it would take some time to reach him. Perhaps an hour. However, with that storm system trailing it might be less than that. Even without the surge of power to move the Pearson 424 he could outrun whatever was coming his way. He took a big swig of his coffee while continuing to watch the scene unfold. He swallowed and moved past the stairs leading down into the boat. Throwing the last of the coffee overboard he dropped the tumbler down below deck and made way to the sails. Plastic hit hard against a stair midway down the steps and ricocheted upwards. An empty thud greeted the quiet cabin as the once filled coffee receptor bounced into the room under his feet.

He gripped a handle and began to let out the main sail. Wind caught strong and he felt the expected push directly away from the storm system. He paused and tied off the sail before letting it out all the way. Curtis walked back to the rear of the ship to get a closer look at what was following him.

From his vantage he still could not make out exactly what it was that was following him. He looked front towards his own vessel and realized he had only clear skies in front of him.

Whatever was moving towards him was not following him intentionally. It was simply moving directly perpendicular to the mass behind it. It was being chased, not him. He looked back towards the horizon with focused purpose and tried hard to evaluate. He could no longer make out any smoke for the dark clouds. In fact, the flame was probably out and only the small outline of a white sail broke the mass like a single star on a dark sky. His adrenaline doubled as Fight or Flight turned quickly to Assist. He made his way back to the sail and pulled hard. The ship swung to port side and fought against his reverse in direction request. As momentum to turn was in his favor, he lowered the sails and brought them all in, all the while broaching towards disaster. With the broadside of the boat geared to take the brunt of the storm Curtis rushed down into the cabin nearly breaking his ankle on the tumbler littering the floor. He pulled cushions from the couch and sought after a hidden door or cabinet or closet. Somewhere he would find the drogue. He knew most ship owners of this vessel's caliber usually purchased everything they could to feel important to the salesperson. Usually they didn't know what everything was but insisted they had it. The interior details of this cabin led him to deduce that the drogue would not be found where it should have been. He was correct. Having been on the more fortunate end of boat theft more often than not, the novice sailor began to get pretty predictable. Especially the wealthy ones.

He finally found it in the restroom tucked in an upper cabinet above the toilet. There were four of them. The Pearson's previous owner obviously liked the price on this sea anchor but wasn't clever enough to buy all the support one needs to successfully deploy it. Or four for that matter.

Nonetheless he quickly carried them all to the deck and made way to upper storage. His ship was trying to right itself and face away from the storm again. He would fix that momentarily. He pulled miles of nylon rope from the storage and displayed it all on the deck. Taking every lifejacket he could find, as well as multiple extra winches, he began his stockpile next to the ropes and drogues.

At the end of the rope he began fixing the winches. There weren't many, but they were heavy. Too heavy to be used on a boat this small, but it didn't seem anyone stopped this guy from buying whatever he wanted to buy. Six winches formed a solid, yet portable, anchor to the end of the rope. Curtis ran off about fifteen yards of nylon and affixed the first drogue. These sea anchors looked like the parachutes that attached to little green army men. In the water they took shape like the obedience cone around a dog leaving the vet. They were light weight, but sturdy. And perhaps too sturdy as Curtis was not in need of being towed in the direction of the current, just steered that way. He pulled a knife from his belt and cut relief into the first drogue. He let out another fifteen yards of nylon and tied on life jackets. Another fifteen yards or so of the nylon and on went more of the heavy winches. Then another drogue with the relief cut into it. Series total was four. Weight, Sea Anchor, Flotation Device. Repeat. Repeat. Repeat.

Curtis made his way to the back of the boat and slowly let the contraption he made into the water. The current was not strong enough to just drop the line in and expect it to catch. He was patient enough to wait for the drogue to fill and start pulling away before he allowed the next series into the water.

Once deployed, this sea anchor chain would fix his position directly facing the storm oncoming. He would be pulled backwards with the force, yet, if the drogues worked as they should, eased down the waves as the pressure would impact the devices more so than the ship. This way he could focus on what was coming towards him and let the storm steer him to always be in its direct line of movement.

Once it was tied off he ensured all his sails were down and secure. Curtis then made his way to the bow of the ship facing the approaching storm and whatever, and whoever, it was bringing with it.

(II)

It was more like falling sideways than sailing. Wrapped around the cracked main mast was the sail. It was folded in half as it had never actually been used before and divided down the middle by the mast it was designed to be attached to. Now just three of the four makeshift corners had been successfully roped down and brought to a focal point to be steered like a giant kite trying to get away. The surviving piece of the deck was no more than thirty feet long and ten feet wide. And there was no symmetry to its design. It simply was just the piece of the ship that was the biggest after the explosion. And now, it was the only remaining piece.

The deck was not designed to be in direct contact with the ocean's surface and certainly was not supposed to be a ship all by itself.

Despite its chaotic transformation from deck to sailboard, it was not in threat of breaking apart so much as it was with tearing loose from the mast. It was not an ideal sailing vessel, but it was getting the job done.

A twenty-five mile per hour wind was about the equivalent of sixty pounds of pull from the sail. This was manageable and about the average coming at the front of this storm system. There were gusts pushing forty miles per hour which put a hefty strain on her small frame, but she was tough. Much more wind than that and she might be lifted up off the deck. It was the lulls in the wind that concerned her the most as she did not want to lose the sail's ability to catch the wind. Working the sail all on her own was tough but stopping was not an option. If it were not for the mast acting as a fulcrum to her pulling, the idle times, few they may be, would have left the sail to crumble like a kite with no spine or crossbar. And no wind. Like a kite with no wind. Just a loose piece of material on a string.

Fortunately, there was plenty of wind as well as a mast for support.

The ropes were digging into her arms already and sitting on the edge facing the storm. With her back to the sail, it was not good for the lower back. Strength from being at sea showed in her powerful legs. Her knees hugged tight over the edge and gripped under the deck. She could feel sea water salting the tiny cuts finding their way to the backs of her legs. She guided the vessel of wreckage along the front of the storm like a wind surfer down the front of a tidal wave. The pressure of holding the sail was not so tremendous right now, but there was question of how long her strength would hold out. It was not the wind and water within the storm that she was worried about, rather the bits and pieces from the man-made menaces to navigation floating around underneath the dark clouds.

Half an hour of this would be about the muscle strain equivalent to riding a bike continuously uphill for five to ten miles. That is when she would let go and let the storm blow by. She had been in a storm for hours and survived in the open sea before, what could possibly be different about this one?

When she felt the wind gusts move to the left or to the right against her rain beaten face, she leaned hard into it pulling the sail to correct its path. The most difficult times were when the wind burst upwards and tried to lift her into the air. The muscle strain would be a distant second on the pain scale of the deepening cuts behind her knees and on the backs of her legs. She would not notice the rope burns on her arms until after a full night's sleep, hopefully coming sooner than later.

Adelle Catrina Jones was a natural in the open sea. She did not mean to blow up the Sambuk they had been traveling in. And even though she had found this sail and these ropes in the middle of the previous night, she really did not intend on having to use them. All she wanted was the currency that she carried in the backpack worn in lieu of a life jacket. Up until an hour ago she did not even think they would notice the missing currency, let alone figure out who she was. Being a woman was her biggest ally. The assumption her reputation built as her being a man was something she did not want to test being proven wrong. Thus far, very few had lived to tell about it once they learned. And those who did know presumed her dead.

Like anyone who survives this would naturally do about everyone else onboard.

Even in the fight against nature now she was wondering who would picture her amongst the dead in this her most recent shipwreck. Unable to think of who really knew where she was, her thoughts began to think of who she could let know.

And how she could let them know without being the one who told them.

Struggling with the wind and the sail, the deck and the sea, as well as the ropes and her torn flesh she fell into a mental peace. Like a runner's high, she felt no pain and just pushed forward.

Fighting to stay on the edge of the storm worked for about five miles. She held together longer than the improvised sailing vessel, and, as she looked up and found herself further within the borders of the wind and rain, everything finally fell apart. The wind pulled upwards and away with such quick force she hadn't the time to brace for it. Without the time to stiffen her legs' grip, she too was yanked from the sanctity of the busted deck and slammed hard into the mast. She and the sail had traded places. Pinned against the large pole she looked upwards along the top of the mast at what she felt she was about to be raked across. It would not be survivable. He arms were pulled tightly backwards with the pressure from the sail. Wasting time trying to cross her arms again would only ensure she was ripped upwards with force. She had to find a way out of the mangled ropes that wrapped her arms and shoulders.

The mast and deck broke loudly near the ocean's surface. A fortunate downward wind change ensured a clean break all because of her as she was the pressure point pinned against the tall beam. As the mast sunk vertically into the ocean the flat deck twisted up on its side. Wind to the sail followed suit and she passed upwards missing the deadly details of the top of the mast, out back towards the edge of the storm like a key on Franklin's kite, and completely airborne. Without the impairment of the mast between her and the sail, her arms were no longer uncomfortably pulled backwards against her body. Like superman flying on his back she had her arms stretched out before her. Grabbing at all the rope she could grip she was able to at least manage a forward feeling direction, even if she had no control at all of where she was being taken. Up was not her concern. It was the eventual down that would be coming soon and where. The heavy mast was likely half a mile below the surface by now, but the deck was lurking below her somewhere.

Jones finally had zero control of the situation. With nothing to concentrate on she stopped her efforts and allowed nature to take over.

(III)

Unless he started the engine, Curtis had no real way of steering the Pearson 424. There was a certain pride about not starting the engine, especially when anyone else would have done so, but he did feel completely helpless being pulled slowly backwards. The waves around him were a solid four to eight feet high. The drogue system seemed to be bringing the roughness to a minimum, but he was not the sailor who was worried about sea-sickness or crashing about. He wanted to control the situation as best as he could.

The sail he could tell had broken loose and he watched it rise quickly for some time, float, then fall back to the sea. He could not imagine how it got loose from the ship the way that it had. Normally you lose just one rope and then have the sail flap untethered like a flag. Like links in a chain, it would be odd to have more than one break. He was close enough to see that it focused back to a point and that it was ripped from somewhere, but he definitely could not make out that it was a person on the end of that errant sail.

The storm had grown wide but was no longer growing in depth. It was a pocket thunderstorm, and if it were not for the previous fire he had seen, the storm would probably not have been much to worry about at all. There was still some significant rain and wind on its way to greet him though, no doubt, but he considered pulling up the sea anchors and redirecting his ship. His experience with shipwrecks usually did not promote need for rescue, and although this storm would be uncomfortable for a survivor, he began to second guess the value of heroism from aboard a stolen sailboat.

The first spots of rain had reached him. Coming in almost sideways and stinging his face. He closed his eyes and allowed the wet to saturate his hair and shirt. Fresh water always tasted so clean with the sweet smell of the ocean accompanying it.

It was much darker when he finally opened his eyes. It hadn't been more than a minute or two. Light shown through the dark clouds here and there, but he was less than a half mile now from the storm itself. In the water around him he began seeing pieces floating by. Something had exploded in the middle of this vast sea. Charred edges of cut wood with forged metal, twisted and soaked, floated by. More and more bits and pieces drifted by on the rising waters as the darkness grew heavier and heavier. The refreshing rain was quickly replaced by an uncomfortable eeriness and sense of urgency. The shortening of his visibility raised his awareness to the complete situation.

Larger pieces began showing up in the mix and the gusts of wind doubled quickly, then doubled again. He moved starboard as the winds had maneuvered the boat a bit counter-clockwise. The drogues pulled him along with the current, not necessarily with the wind directly.

Coming down the near side of a steep wave he saw it. It reflected like the flat well-polished surface of a ship's deck. Waves blocked his view and he rose to his tip toes with no reward. The P424 then began to rise upon its own wave and he paused eagerly waiting to see what would prove to be the most intact piece coming from the wreckage.

It was the deck. And there was someone on top of it.

He was still unable to coerce his ship one way or the other. To leave now and start the engines would surely result in his losing sight of the thing. The deck. The person. He inched along the railing like the point on a compass facing where he wished he was moving towards. Fortunately, the float was ultimately being carried by the same current he was being moved by. Although there was an odd angle to it, the two moving vessels did have a constant bearing towards each other. Curtis merely had to find the patience for the range between them to decrease.

The gap closed quickly, and he was able to confirm that there was someone on top of the floating dance floor. The low profile of the deck and the angle of the side of his boat did not make for a proper collision. The P424 would soon glide right over whatever, and whoever, was on the deck. He began hollering with all his might. It was difficult for the storm, but he could not stop. Throwing his voice out towards the sea nearly pulled him overboard. Rain found a way to soak deeper into his hair and clothes and skin. Lightning both assisted and ruined his visibility and he never could predict where the next bolt would be.

Waves became stronger than the current moving the sea anchors and the Pearson was pushed more and more counter-clockwise. Without realizing it, he had crept towards the rear of the boat and had lost most practical use of the system he had flowing under the surface of the sea. The deck of the broken Sambuk was nearly upon the starboard side.

His screaming stopped right before impact. Under the boat it slid as it came down the wave that his boat was going up. The body lay unmoving as the force cracked the deck in two.

Jones plummeted into the ocean and was greeted by a harsh reality.

Curtis was not so ignorant of the ocean that he would jump in. He still did not know if the body was of the living or not. As the halved deck tried to bob back to life on the surface, the splashing of arms and faint intermittent cries made it to him. Running into the much smaller boat piece did not have a dramatic effect on the intact Pearson 424, but Newton's Third still held true. He now was finally at the back of the boat as it had completed a full about face from when he was originally facing the oncoming storm.

Some thirty feet out he could see a bundle of life vests floating. He gripped the nylon rope tied to the back of the boat's rails. Pulling the sea anchor in was a futile attempt against this sea but he could do little else from his petty vantage. He thought he could somehow guide the floating line towards the fallen sailor.

Jones could not see the line near her, nor could she see the boat it was connected to. Vision was not the major sense she was most concerned with. All she wanted to ensure was that she was not inhaling sea water. Yet more than that was her constant awareness of the bag around her shoulders.

The body in the water neared the sea anchor system and Curtis stared with his mouth agape and eyes darting from vests to swimmer. Despite the violence of the waves for the storm, the splashing was still noticeable. Strength from somewhere kept her swimming even after her bought with the sail and the wind. Finally, an arm went over the rope in the water and she opened her eyes wider than ever before. She looked up towards the boat and Curtis first realized it was a woman. She only saw the boat and trusted that the rope she had found was attached to the floating object before her. She pulled herself no more than ten feet up the nylon against the waves before she found the middle set of life vests in the chain. She could pull no more.

Jones shoved her arms down into the floating nest and gave up. Curtis immediately leapt from the back of his boat and crashed awkwardly into the rising and falling waves below. He fought to find the rope and began to pull himself out and away from the boat. It seemed forever before he made the length to where she had affixed herself and he spun the web of vests towards him so that he could pull her out. Without strength she looked over at him and closed her eyes again. He threw an arm under hers and began pulling with his other arm. Fishing for some grip with his feet and legs and continued to move slowly back towards the boat.

At last the nylon fully surfaced and stretched upwards towards the rear of the Pearson424. They were fortunate the waves now pushed the boat forwards and wasn't a complete threat of crushing them. The crests at times brought the boat only some 4 feet from the surface, while at its peak the deck towered twelve feet above from the top of a ten-foot wave.

Curtis maneuvered the woman in front of him and began to look for a way to hold her and climb upwards. He grabbed a strap from the backpack she was wearing and started to remove it.

Jones clinched her jaw and opened her eyes. Turning her shoulder away in the midst of the crashing waves she grabbed Curtis about the wrist. The movement dropped her below the water surface and her gripped tightened as it suddenly became all that she had. He grabbed the nylon with both hands to avoid being pulled under. He no longer cared about the backpack.

She rose grasping for air and reached for the rope while never letting go of his wrist. Both of them pulled themselves against their arms clinching the rope just above the ocean's surface. She was wide awake, and Curtis could see the fight in her eyes.

"Whatever you do" he began as he let go and reached back towards the knife in his belt, "don't let go."

As he cut the rope as far away from their grips as he could, the two of them were pulled towards the back of the Pearson and right up against it. He leaned back holding the rope and put his feet against the hull to avoid hitting the side again. Jones slid down the rope a piece and found the new end with one hand and looped it up back towards her other hand. She hitched the end back onto the rope and created a loop.

"Climb God damn it!" she screamed before a salty wave doused her for what seemed the millionth time. She put her foot in the loop and tried to steer her shoulder under his foot. As he adjusted and completed her request she pushed into the loop forcing him up the rope and out of the ocean. The next eight or nine feet to the railing was up to him.

He was up to the task. He gripped the nylon rope above his head with one hand like he was slowly running in place. Pulling down on the rope he repeated the action with the other side. His feet and legs were useless against this rope of little friction. He kicked at the boat as often as momentum allowed. Six difficult pulls got him to where he needed to be and as he swung himself to safety he began to pull Jones up. She gathered the rope above her while she kept her foot in the loop for safety. Finally, he could reach her arm and as she grabbed back at him the rope fell back down like a tiny tail on a giant elephant. He pulled her over and away from the waves.

They fell upon the deck with Curtis smothering her. He began to push himself up with apology and paused less than half a foot from her as she opened her eyes.

Her green eyes cut through the rain. He hesitated to move. She swallowed and while inhaling quietly mouthed "thank you."

Curtis and Jones had no hesitation left. Even without strength to move again, they found it. He returned from pushing away to meet his lips with hers. New strength overcame Jones as she pushed him over and was immediately straddling over him. He started to return the favor when she leaned over and pushed his shoulders back against the deck. One hand moved quickly up away from him and she found his lips once more. His hands gripped her below the rib cage and his fingers struck at the backpack that now carried mostly water. She leaned back and pulled the backpack's straps from her shoulders. Looking left she spotted the opening for the lower cabin and flung the pack of money, guaranteeing its security, down the steps. In the same glance back to Curtis she found the bottom of her torn shirt and pulled it over her head. Curtis leaned up, grabbed her around her bare waste, turned and pinned her again to the deck. He brought one knee up, rose slightly away from Jones and pulled his shirt away. She grabbed at his belt and pulled the front of it towards her. As he fell towards the side of her neck and put his lips to the bottom of her earlobe she loosened his belt with the hand that remained upon it.

"Fuck me" she moaned towards his ear. His pants tightening already, Curtis stood and unfastened what she had not yet and pulled what clothing he had left over his feet quickly. She had unbuttoned her pants already and he gripped them and her panties near her hips and, as she lifted the small of her back off the deck, he pulled her wet clothes off.

Without hesitation he fell back towards her. His left elbow up above her shoulder and his right arm down aside her side, he drew his hips back to position himself and entered inside of her. As his eyes closed with passion hers opened. He leaned his head back and began to push harder, forcing himself fully into the woman he had just saved. She reached down and grabbed his ass pulling him into her as though he wasn't trying hard enough. He reopened his eyes to meet hers. Even at night during a storm he saw their green intensity coming right back to him. He began to withdraw from her and forced himself right back. Each time she felt him thrust into her was harder than the last.

Jones wrapped her legs around Curtis' hips and back behind him. She twisted and again found herself on top of the now naked hero that had just pulled her from the ocean. She reached back to unclasp her bra.

Curtis was motionless as her wet hair fell wet to one side from her after their latest transposition of places. With her arms back to unhook the last piece of clothing either of them wore, he felt his cock grow harder while still deep inside of her. She pulled her bra off.

She was quite petite overall, but her full breasts set perfectly upon her as she leaned in and put her hands on his chest. The movement pushed her tits together even more as she leaned back and rocked her hips.

It wasn't enough for her. She leaned to a side and pulled Curtis back over on top of her. He willingly made what would be their final transition. As he was again mounted above her, he looked down at her breasts as they naturally flattened against her body. Fucking her hard now, he moved from watching the movement of her perfect breasts to her, and her eyes staring right back at him. Her eyes had him pushing harder than his body should have allowed and as she closed her eyes and leaned her head back, he began to come.

Jones for the first time in her sexual life had a silent, yet still the largest, orgasm of her life. Curtis came hard, as deep inside of her as he was physically capable of.

Exhaustion had finally won its hard-fought battle against them. They both slept, Curtis Scott and "The Cat" Jones, as they were, he inside of her, on top of that boat deck, and in the passing storm.

MAR CANTÁBRICO

A small sea that feeds a vast sea.

(I)

I was one of three that slept in the break room. All present had been here before. The tingling of my left foot woke me up and I knew immediately if I pulled it from the table too quickly my entire leg would go numb. My foot went numb just as an 'I told you so.' Falling backwards from the chair and having gravity waking me up would have been the greater of the two evils. I guess it was still gravity that got the credit for waking me as the blood in my leg was not able to climb up and feed my foot. I leaned forward and lifted my leg from the table bringing it down to the floor. Straight out in front of me I felt the blood flow release. From the top of my knee the rush was like a cheap water park and the teenager-manned soda straws put my blood on the fast track to the murky-watered foot pool at the end of my shin. The familiar pain was excruciating.

It would not be the worst pain I felt today, but easily the second worse.

The pain in my leg was loud enough it seemed strange to have not awoken my travel partners in the same room. I knew standing would quicken the pain of having a sleeping limb come alive again, but it would also quicken the whole natural ordeal. I limped to the stairway and gingerly made my way up to the deck.

Swansea was up walking the deck already. I couldn't see him, but knew he was there somewhere. I paused and waited for a moment and then smelled tobacco from the ends of a cigarette. I walked upwind to find him. Despite his aromatic declaration of location, being upwind, and the comfort of walking the deck alone for years, it still felt as though he knew of my presence before I knew of his.

He was not trying to be sneaky, he just had his way. I passed him by about three whole feet before he stepped closer to me. I greeted him with a glance and a slowed pace.

I don't know that he ever really greeted me in return. He just kind of stopped in my general area as though I was a natural element of the terrain. Like walking a path in the woods and coming across a tree. He was towards the end of his cigarette. It looked like the first two knuckles of his left hand were glowing. He smoked like a poor man who really wasn't sure how he was going to support his nicotine habit. He burned each cigarette down to the filter, every time. The final exhale of thick smoke seemed filled with thankfulness and hope.

He crushed the cigarette butt with an iron clench of his fist, simultaneously smothering it and rolling it into a compact ball. He looked over as though we had just finished a long conversation. I felt as though Swansea and I had had more wordless conversations than monks on a dual 40-day vow of silence and a fast of strong ale.

"They aim to kill you." He said to me point blank as though it was as common as 'good morning'. "This ship will be sunk just before we enter Gibraltar. If you speak of it, you'll be killed beforehand. I'd like to ensure you have a fighting chance." He paused to allow for me to speak. I didn't. "A fighting chance means you live another day, not fight to save anyone. You understand?"

I responded as only he would have.

He pulled at his inside coat pocket for his pack of smokes. He deftly shook the pack and offered the lone protruding cigarette to me. I took it. He shook the pack again and put the new butt in his mouth directly. Replacing the pack, he produced a lighter and lit his own cigarette in the same motion as he was handing me the lighter.

I struggled to light my own and prayed I would look comfortable smoking.

"There will be a celebration of arrival and you'll need to not participate. The beer is tainted and will put us all to sleep so they can sabotage the boat. I've shown them how to produce a mechanical failure that won't be questioned." He spat.

"Is it safe for me to find rescuers or do I need to get to shore on my own?" I asked breaking the sound barrier for the first time today.

"Get to the Spanish side for certain. And find your way to Lisbon, cause Spain ain't safe for you without proper identification. There you'll find safe passage back to Liverpool. And be sure Liverpool is your first destination. You'll know what to do there. Then whatever you do is up to you. I know you'll be fine."

And that was the end of the conversation.

I don't know why he gave me the heads up. I don't know who I should look for in Lisbon or even how to get there. I certainly am trying to doubt my knowledge of what to do in Liverpool and I have no idea if he'll be drinking the beer or when. I certainly feel not following his quiet words to the letter will not fit well for my future.

Had he been waiting for me? Would he have found the time to tell me if I didn't show up for a conversation this morning? Was I the only one he would be telling? I feel like I should not care so much and just go with it. Accept what has been given to me and take care of myself. I wasn't dealt a winning hand, but it was strong enough to ensure I pushed.

Swansea moved towards the other end of the boat, checking everything as though it was not about to be sunk in the next twelve hours. I made my way towards the bow.

Off about a quarter of a mile was a large pod of sea creatures. Dolphins would have been closer to the ship playing in the wake. As I looked down towards where the dolphins would've been if it were, I saw a single dolphin-like creature swimming towards the other grouping. It was much larger than a dolphin but moved closer to what I expected a whale to move like. They were moving faster than this large barge was and more westerly towards the Atlantic than the shore.

The stir of life was brewing below the deck as well. I could feel it. It felt like their last day alive.

Not just Swansea's crew, all of them.

The bright moonlight would soon be covered by the sun which would eventually be replaced by the sea. I looked up and gazed wishing I had coffee. I pushed my fingers through my thickening beard and found some skin to scratch.

(II)

I was surprised to see the non-veterans arrive on deck first. I tried not to think too much about what their escape plan was as it seemed they knew my thoughts. So, I just maintained my path back underdeck to ready with the rest of my guys. They literally passed me on the way down and I felt like I was late for work already. They didn't care. If they did know, it wouldn't be anything they held against me for too much longer anyway.

I must have been staring at that pod of giant dolphins for longer than I had thought. Strange to think that if I had spent that much time deep in thought I might have thought of something. I couldn't remember a god damn thing.

I felt the obligation of being behind on time, yet simultaneously the calm of forever and ultimate knowledge. I found the coffee and poured myself a cup before retreating to my bunk to change out of yesterday's socks. I looked around the cabin we shared to see if I needed to prepare for anything to be easily reached. I wonder how many people got the opportunity to plan for a disaster before it happened. Then I thought of Swansea.

You don't have to get ready if you're already ready.

I pulled my passport from deep within my bag and looked it over. The last stamp it had on it was from my arrival in the UK. I didn't spend too much time in front of a mirror anymore, but I couldn't help but think how much I did not resemble this man I saw in the picture. I touched my cheeks. They certainly did not feel as plumb as they looked. I tucked the legal document into a pocket and put my bag close to the doorway just in case I could make it back in time for it.

There was nothing else here I needed. I made myself comfortable for the day and made my way up to help the boys. There wouldn't really be much to do for the duration of the day. Everything was set and all hands were on deck to secure anything that might come loose.

CIRCLE OF QUIESCENCE

Constancy and perpetual motion.

(I)

Calm waters and steady wind were not the norm this far out at sea. Neither was sleeping on the deck of a boat after a windfall encounter. Curtis' internal compass startled him awake and he looked off towards the sun rising in the east.

"Let's get the sails up" she was no more than ten feet from him starboard, "assuming you want to go South and not farther West." As soon as he moved to hoist the sails she followed to accompany him. Their teamwork was nearly flawless. In less than ten minutes the two of them had the Pearson 424 headed South-Southeast and back along the path towards the Straits of Gibraltar.

Neither Curtis nor Cat Jones pressed the issue of what happened the night before. They both knew and they both had the tedious task of going about a normal day after a traumatic event. They were trapped in the fog following a car accident, or sudden loss of a family member. Traffic would just keep passing you by, office workers would keep sending out emails and the grocery checker would still be there wondering when six o'clock would come so she could get off from work.

The wind would keep blowing and the sea would keep turning over and over. Storms do not hunt down ships and waves do not seek out to crash. But once they do, they keep on moving, whether or not anyone along the way notices or not.

Both of them had been through wreckage before and many times had been the instigators. This encounter was different. As the ship was righted along the path that Curtis intended he made his way down to start some coffee. She followed.

He had a couple weeks and some serious hours logged into this ship, but it was not that much more familiar to him than it was to her. Had the décor not clued her in already, his struggle to find her a drinking device was a good indicator this ship was new to him. While he searched the coffee brewed and she looked over a small book shelf. It felt more ornamental than functional as she lifted a once opened, never read, book about the Battle of Hastings. She read the inscription on the first blank page 'knowing your side of the battle is the first step for pride' which was signed only with the name Willows. She slowly closed the book and looked around the room while trying to remember.

"It was a source of shame to some that we have no recorded ancestors on either side of the Battle of Hastings" she narrated while placing the book down likely to never be opened again. Curtis was reaching into an upper cabinet hoping to score a container of some sort as there was no thermos that he could locate. He only assumed she was of the type that preferred her coffee to stay as hot as possible for as long as possible. He never once questioned if she even liked coffee, that was simply a given in his world.

"Look like a good book?" he asked without a care wishing instantly that he cared. He stopped and gave his attention to his guest. "Doing a little light reading?" he asked trying to sound a little more pleasant to the woman he had been inside of just under half a day before.

She was masking a bit of anxiety trying to sound smart and quickly realized she should be more straight-forward to her rescuer than so tart. "The book is dedicated to Willows, or I guess I should say 'from' Willows..." she found the name above the stairwell leading to the deck above and motioned to it. Curtis looked over at a detail he had never seen before. She continued, "my guess it is *your* last name?"

"Nope, Scott. Curtis Scott" and he walked over to formally meet the redheaded gem, half dressed, ignoring the cold set deep within her bones, and standing boldly within a random ship out in the sea.

"Jones" she replied, and the two ship-weathered hands met like real people meet. "So, Willows is just the name of the person you took the boat from?" she questioned knowingly.

"Must be" said Curtis as he looked at the curves along the ornate lettering above the stairwell. His eyes followed each letter as the surname burned into his mind like a sparkler during a holiday. He turned back to her, "but you never really know those things, y'know?" a pause between them for acknowledgment before he got to the point, "coffee?"

She nodded enthusiastically while smirking away the need for the question.

"'It was a source of shame to some that we have no recorded ancestors on either side of the Battle of Hastings'" she repeated. "... That book was about the Battle, but the inscription referenced pride and this boat's *former* owner's name." she began.

Curtis was not the well-read scholar, "so if it was about pride, then why were they shameful to not be represented at some battle?"

"No, it seems they were represented. The inscription in the book was about pride and *knowing* they were represented. The quote about shame is from 'To Kill A Mockingbird'." She suddenly wished they were talking about how he stole this boat. She noted more things around the den that were obviously not from this lean, well-built twenty-something Irishman. Though considering he probably was sailing from his hometown, she was impressed he kept the cabin as tidy as it was.

Curtis began pouring coffee, "That's the book with Atticus, Boo Radley and... Scout. Yes?"

"Did you read the book or just see the movie?" she tossed back playfully, happy he was at least catching the reference and not leaving her feeling like a know-it-all.

"Neither. You just pick up things along the way I guess." He handed her a carafe of coffee and motioned towards the stairs and the name above it, "think Mr. Willows would mind if we took to the deck?"

They started up and he continued, "so which side were they on for the Battle of Hastings?"

"The side chosen was not the point…"

"So, you don't know which side?" He quipped back trying to get ahead in the conversation.

"No, I don't" she deflected argument with her tone, "however it really was about tradition, and knowing that you belonged to a side. Apparently, the Willows family was proud that they had taken a side in the battle, but I didn't read into it far enough to see which side they took."

"Well I don't take sides" he said proudly as they approached the deck where they had lain the night before.

"Just boats then?"

"Yes" he smiled, "and beautiful maidens floating out in the sea after shipwreck."

She felt the warm blood fill her cheeks and she remembered flying through the air on a sail. Suddenly the muscle ache in her legs was as real as the memory had just been. "Do you slay dragons, too, Mr. Scott?"

"Curtis." He looked away from her and off towards the East where land would show in the next twenty-four hours, "and only the wooden ones."

He had no idea who she was or where she came from. He didn't ask if she was ok or if there were anyone else they should be looking for. He took no sides and kept to himself, knowing only that he needed to get to the Strait of Gibraltar. Knowing that he was supposed to arrive alone. Knowing that he didn't want to really do anything alone. At least not this day.

Curtis Scott confidently took the wheel, leaving Jones to take a back seat. It was up to him, or the wind, to take her where they may.

(II)

Rising slowly from over one-thousand feet below the ocean's surface, it had been nearly an hour since his dive. A belly full of fish, squid and the major pieces of a giant squid left to die and fall to the bottom of the sea; the bull whale was finally re-entering waters with some visibility. With no sense of urgency to get to the surface, echolocation begins to locate his pod. Being the eldest, his head white with age against his dark grey-brown body, he was more announcing his return to the surface from a feast than an attempt to find them.

Still drifting down towards the ocean's floor was an adolescent giant squid, one eye in the belly and the other ruptured from the two protruding lower teeth of its attacker, its defense was ill-prepared. Its tentacles, now five fewer remaining on the leftover piece of its body, did their part to scratch at the bull whale but merely added a trivial few more cuts to its already scarred skin.

With relatively small flippers for a whale, and a beaked nose like a goose, he resembled a giant dolphin more so than a whale. Pride was not an emotion felt during this slow climb to the surface. Just another feeding day. It was usually the larger sperm whales that could battle against a giant squid. This beaked-whale did not seek them out, but at these depths he had encountered a few over the past forty-some years of life at sea.

Twelve other whales of the same species traveled together and, although they were not all of the same family directly, they had been together for decades over multiple generations. This particular bull was indeed the eldest, the largest and the most aggressive, but preferred to hunt alone and at a much deeper level under sea than the rest. He had only sired one calf and did not know which of the pod it was, but it made no matter, they were all part of his family.

Hunting in the deep waters was particularly successful west of the Spanish coast. The warm waters flowing north from the Mediterranean finally rose towards the surface after its push into the depths of the Atlantic Ocean. The southern moving cold waters weighed heavy along the ocean's floor stirring up much of the bottom dwellers. These low sailing fish feasted well along the ever-moving floor but were also victim to the deep diving maneuvers of a beaked whale pod. Hammerheads, ground sharks and other predators of the deep sea had to make way as the dolphin-looking giants came crashing into the ground around them. Rays, eels and every sunken fish waiting out its own prey are forced out of hiding and into the demise of the wolf-like tactics of the whales.

Desperate to get back to the ground level after their comfort had been dismantled by the battering ram style methods of the giant hunters, most of the displaced fish are sucked up by the very beasts that crashed the ocean floor. Above them await the rest of the whale pod who capture the oily-livered bottom dwellers who felt swimming up and away from danger was the better choice.

The hunting pod will crash and raid the ocean's bottom until their fill has been made. Exhausted and full they settle to the surface together anticipating their elder's arrival and familiar song. Almost twenty feet long he slows to an even more measured pace as he arrives at the surface for one of the few breaths he'll take before the sun is at its fullest. The spray blows out releasing the mammal's lung capacity no higher than a doorknob from a threshold. Still without hast the beast draws in fresh air only after his lungs are emptied of the waste he's been creating below the surface. He immediately dives again until he finds comfort at about thirty feet below the gentle waves above him.

Most of the beaked whales maintain just under the water while the two youngest calves keep their backs and dorsal fins out in the sun. Those two are mostly white while the rest are grey and dark grey. Only the eldest bull deepest below the surface has grown into his browner skin. Seemingly reclusive, they are actually quite social. As with any intelligent group that is around each other day in and day out, they mostly mind to themselves and simply maintain a close proximity. Anytime another whale pod, same species or not, is nearby and can be heard or felt, they at least respond. Many times, the pods will cross paths and, on occasion, they will lose a member or gain a member during the mingling.

The males have two elongated teeth on their lower jaws that are for fighting, usually over females. The deep scratches along their thick skin are displayed for the world as evidence. Their pointed heads give no sign of a neck as their bodies are dense and streamlined to allow for a deeper, longer dive into the depths of the ocean. Males do not necessarily outweigh the females, though the elders are the largest members of the group. The more mature of the group also employ the better hunting methods and tend to get the bigger meals, even when others attempt to share them. Here in the ocean, in this aquatic jungle, the prey is consumed outright and not left along the terrain to be shared by the family. About half a year after birth, every member of the family is on its own. Cows cannot coddle their calves and take their share of a school of fish leaving the rest for the growing whale. Fish that don't get caught just keep swimming.

None lead and all follow. There is no rhyme or reason to the order that this herd will travel in as all but the youngest know the way. They maintain a Southwestern movement feeling the cool waters at their back and warm waters rising and leading them down their path. The farther from the shore they move the farther away the ocean's floor becomes. The cold Canary Current will finally dominate the outrush of the Mediterranean and guide them to the equator. The pod will follow these currents south, then west along the equator and back up until they are met with the fierce rush of the Gulf Stream near the North American coast and cycle back to the waters surrounding Ireland and England once again.

They pass under a boat that is twice as large as their eldest member. The group's disinterest for things along the surface and their enormous oxygen capacity allows them to simply dive a little deeper and move along mostly unnoticed. They had done this countless times and would be back here within another year.

(III)

"Those aren't dolphins." Curtis stated while overlooking the bow of the forty-two-foot-long sailing vessel. It was almost more of a question than a statement, but his tone left enough for him to side on whichever was closer to correct.

"Whales." Cat Jones instructed as she sipped her coffee. None of them moving or even hinting towards progressing the conversation.

Curtis stood slowly in thought. He looked up above the horizon and towards the sky with his eyes squinting, "but they're little whales… right?" He no longer cared about which side of the conversation he was on; these whales did not look right to him.

"They're twenty feet long! How do you mean they're *little* whales?"

"They're not more than ten feet long, fifteen the longest one" and he looked back down into the depths trying to find the one whale he was talking about amongst the similar creatures deep below. "Shit how can you even tell they're all so far under the water?"

"Exactly." And she let her point linger hoping he had enough of his own point to prove hers outright.

She gazed at him while he stared into the ocean deep in thought. Finally, he could think about it no longer, "how long are they?"

"At least twenty feet." She pointed hard, "That one is so far under the water it must be massive."

"I've seen bigger." He stated as if that proved any point about the whales.

"Not every whale is a blue whale."

"So, what are these? Dwarf whales?" He said all too seriously as she punched him in his shoulder.

"No, just giant fucking dolphins."

He nodded in agreement much to her displeasure and they both settled back into watching the pod move farther and farther out of sight.

Due east on the horizon there was a slow-moving vessel headed south. Curtis finally caught sight of it and decided he was likely closer to land, Portugal or even Gibraltar, than he had anticipated. He needed to start making the turn towards the Southeast sooner than later. He needed to figure out what to do with his stowaway. She already pinned him for a boat thief, so he didn't figure letting her know she wasn't supposed to be with him would be much of a surprise.

He couldn't take his eyes off the silhouette of the distant ship he knew he would see up close in the next few hours as they caught up to them.

"Baby whales." He said conclusively as he passed her by on his way for more coffee.

Jones closed her eyes and shook her head. She was filled with a growing admiration for the reality of this particular prince charming. Her joy was the deepest of her emotions. It was not the easiest to see looking upon the surface of her face, but it was there; commanding, mature and a major part of everything and nothing all at once. She knew what was important and what was to be kept within. Where the power was and when to have it, when to show it, and when it mattered most.

She also knew when to be soft and when she just needed to be a woman. The emotions that needed to be seen where the ones she let drift near the surface and bask in the warmth of the sun. Those that were the strongest often lead the way from deep within. Her passion was in the sea and that is where she spent the majority of her time. Lost within its depth and rarely ever coming up to the surface and exposing herself to the outer elements, she was home here. But even the oldest, wisest and most stubborn of us all still need companionship.

She gazed into the ocean where the whales had been long after their journey took them beyond her little place in the world. She went down to the kitchen with the assumption that the coffee had long been made and ready. She found that it had and poured herself a cup. Curtis was out of the common rooms of the cabin.

Hoping to find a taste of the spark they had on the deck after they first met, she went looking for him. The bathroom door in the hall was open proving he was not there so Jones made her way to the bedroom. He was talking to himself in the small shower tucked into a corner of the room build around the king-sized bed. No water running, Curtis was half lathered in soap having what seemed to be a normal conversation, only without anyone to converse with.

"I imagine you're finding a way to lose both sides of this argument" she announced. Still hoping for some wayward romance, she couldn't help but notice there was absolutely no water running and he continued to soap himself.

"I didn't realize I had been talking out loud" he said honestly as he successfully masked his alarm at being caught in the nude. "and these are really the only moments that I lose a conversation."

"There isn't any water running, are we running low? You make coffee like there is plenty of water stored on this boat."

"We've got plenty of water. Why?"

She was dumbfounded by the question and looked at him appropriately so. The hope for a second splash with this lost sailor fading quickly, but for no fault of the situation. The passion came from the moment, not the person, and she accepted. He was not someone she would spend the rest of her life with, at least not lovingly.

Curtis would, however, spend the rest of his life with her.

"Old habits" he said pointing to the water spout on the opposite side of the shower from him like it was the plumbing's fault. "I've always just used water when I needed to. Surrounded by the seawater so often I just don't take fresh water for granted." He shrugged playfully, never really having had to explain himself enough to really think about it before.

"So, coffee is a necessity?"

He nodded with confident urgency and watched her calmly smile for the first real time since they met. Her now childish eyes looked his soapy body over once and she raised her eyebrows at him when she found his face again. Her longing for lust successfully passed over to him as she walked away content with the relationship that was building with him.

It wasn't until she was out of his sight that he thought the moment could have turned into something more. He remembered her body like it was something out of a dream and was willing, very willing, to taint those memories with the everyday details. She was no book to be judged by its cover. Curtis even had the opportunity to be a major player in a chapter of her book, but still that was not enough to understand the novel.

He thought that even if she had told him true all the stories that she had he would never be able to unravel the masterpiece that she was. As he turned the water back on to wash off he thought perhaps that was true for everyone.

They would speak few words as they made and ate breakfast, sipped coffee and enjoyed the ever-steady increase in the wind as they gained ground on the shipping boat headed into The Straits of Gibraltar.

BREAKING SOLITUDE

Moving beyond the self and towards the all-encompassing.

(I)

I didn't anticipate the explosion. It came from deep within the ship's hull and although I knew something was going to happen, I still wasn't quite ready for it. I never saw any of them make a move towards sabotage. I never caught them looking worried, triumphant or deviant. I never witnessed anything out of the ordinary.

They had been robotic. Set in their ways and focused on their mission. Without incident they had begun their coordinated mayhem and they had yet to bat an eye. The crew looked stymied as their routine had been reduced to nothing. It wasn't something they had felt move beneath them before.

Swansea had the finest crew based on collective years at sea. Myself definitely not included. They had weathered many storms, natural and otherwise, but the boat had never moved below their feet the way it just had. They could each work on a motor and knew the ship's movements based on ailment. Normally it was just a slow in movement, sometimes preceded by a sudden jolt forward, but never anything that shot them sideways. Especially not without a giant wave crashing over the side, but even then, it was never a singular unexpected wave.

Modern piracy didn't have them attacked first as the pirates would want to board the ship and plunder, take hostage, or just remove the crew and take the vessel outright. This was, however, the general exclamation coming from them all until it was finally declared that this came from within the ship, not from without.

At that they stopped clamoring trying to look over the side at the gaping hole that was now a prominent feature of the cargo carrier. Down towards the engine room they all rushed. And behind them, seemingly right to plan, the scallywags followed them down. I made my way to the captain's quarters only to find the door locked from the inside. From this vantage point I could see quite a few things; two empty cargo ships coming from the east, a single sailboat coming from the west, and that the freight aboard this boat was not entirely secure. Also knowing how loud the radio was, I was surprised not hearing it. No signal had been sent to alert of any danger and I was certain Swansea was on the other side of the door.

I made my way back down to the deck and headed towards the stairwell leading to the motor. Three of them were on their way back up as I began my way down. One was carrying a broken pipe.

"What can I do to help?" I pretended, moving to the side to allow them all back up.

"Just go see what you can do." And I was allowed down into what was assumed my final resting place. I wondered if they would seal the entrance once we were all down here. If so, this would be a straight forward excursion on my part, but I heard no attempt at the top of the stairs as I headed down farther below the ship's deck. All the hallways were filled with thick grey smoke. I was ready to be bludgeoned at any moment but continued into the belly of the boat to see what I could do. At this point, no one was going to save the motor and no one was going to save the crew.

Entering the large room that housed the motor, I saw the hole in the side of the ship first before I saw fighting. Swansea's men were tough, but they were no match for these bullies. Two were already on the ground being surrounded by the fast-moving water coming in from the couch sized rip in the wall. They had pipes that seemed to have broken off from the motor itself while the men were punching in desperation trying to avoid more broken bones. The bones would break, and it seemed as though that was the intent. Like giant cats playing with wounded mice, the true sailors fought against these men with their arms and ribs in tatters. Never once did a blow to the head occur, and their legs were not struck until the water was passed knee level. I was no match for these weapon-yielding killers.

My arm was grabbed, and I was pulled back into the entryway. Swansea had been in the room, probably setting the explosion himself, but was not participating in either side of the fight.

"What the fuck are you doing down here? I told you no heroes." I saw fear in his eyes, but not the kind of fear that ran from its problems, just the uncertain kind. He had never put his men at risk before, at least not intentionally.

I pulled the passport from my pocket and held it up for him to see then I dropped it into the rising water.

"I'm escaping." I left the killers there to continue pummeling the men. Apparently, it had to look like they had been beaten badly by the motor and the constant thrusting back and forth of the sea.

Swansea and I rushed back towards the deck and found that the path had not been locked, but rather blocked. Of course, why in a disaster would the door be locked when the same results could come about from locking the door behind us as it could lodging crates down the same entryway.

"They're unloading the boxes up there." He said before I could make out the sound of the onboard cranes scraping the large freight boxes along the deck.

One by one they dropped them overboard as the ship took on more water. Our only way out was through the room with the carnage. With multi-tons crates being unloaded on the far side of the ship, and a hole on this side of the ship, we were quickly learning that our side would soon be the bottom of the ship. I did my best to rush through the now shin-deep water in the room.

There were three of them and it started to seem far too familiar. Their focus was not on me, but at the task at hand. Pummeling this ship's crew. I shoved one of them as he struck a man again. He fell off balanced and took a knee in the water before looking back at me. Swansea's team still had some fight and he grabbed at the fallen man's throat. I kick him in the stomach to make the strangulation that much more intense. I lifted the pipe from his grip and left him to his now-former victim's assault.

I was not unnoticed at this point.

Two of them remained and I was now their focus. New life surged through their once tired veins as beating men seemed to only temporarily tire them. I was scared but had to get myself and Swansea out of that hole and into the sea. I looked to my side to check on Swansea's whereabouts and caught a glimpse of him helping to finish the first attacker we encountered.

I was on my own with these two. At least until I could get some help from the badly beaten men crouched down in the water.

If they could even get up.

The man closest to me started to swing and I had to make a quick reaction. I tucked in like a downhill skier and allowed the force to crash into my left arm. He didn't swing the pipe like a baseball bat, this man swung the pipe like he had been swinging pipes and other random objects for their own sport. It would have been senseless to try and kick with the thickness of the water slowing down my momentum, so I lunged for him and tried to use the water as a tool. I kept him between myself and the second assailant. I didn't want to have to deal with more than one at a time if I could help it. I punched at his face and head, landing less than half of what I threw out. However, I did succeed in keeping his focus from swinging that god damn pipe again. I finally worked my left hand over to grabbing at his weapon while maintaining a steady attack with my right. He never considered letting the pipe go, but it would have made things so much simpler.

With him still between myself and the next, I pushed. I pushed as hard as I could, and the water maintained its place stopping his lower half from moving as quickly as his upper half. It did the same for me and I ended up falling over towards him. Also closer towards the swinging distance of the other man.

He didn't hesitate.

Instantly my left arm was struck again. This one felt like it had some anger behind it. It was followed quickly by another and when a third came for my head I ducked. I ducked right into the man below me catching his lower jaw as he was taking in a deep breath rising from the deepening waters. It did not look comfortable as his chin made its way to his chest.

I pushed myself up and drove my legs. He swung backwards after quickly adjusting his momentum and managed to find contact with my head. I was fortunate it was a less than powerful backswing, like a tennis player doing their best to serve with their non-dominant hand.

It still hurt, but I was moving quickly now. I raised my right arm up to the left and used the impact to turn myself and grab around both of his arms with my strongest arm. I found myself almost behind him as a spun into hold him and was at a loss for what to do next.

I bit him hard in the throat. His head came crashing into my own head and I could feel his teeth against my temple. His attempt would not match my success. The copper flavored blood dominated my mouth as a chunk of his throat lost its placement. I could smell the blood when I exhaled through my nose. It reminded me of getting drunk on butterscotch schnapps as a teenager and vowing never to touch the stuff again after a night and a morning of vomiting the sugary stuff up.

I hoped to never bite into someone's neck again.

I looked like a character from a bad vampire movie. The heavy pipe made nearly the same splash as he did when he hit the water below. Mainly because it was up to our thighs now.

117

Two men and Swansea had the man I had headbutted and were holding him under for a quick death. He was fine. They were not. In fact, they were doing a good job of using their broken limbs, however their adrenaline would not keep up long enough to help them swim for very long.

Four of us made it out of the hole and into the sea. The ship was turning towards us as the deck had mostly been cleared of the large crates. Each of which was floating about on the opposite side of the ship waiting for the arriving boats to pluck them out of the water. I would have been surprised to see anyone come this side looking for their comrades. By the way these guys worked, had one of them survived to be swimming about right now, they too would probably have been surprised to see someone looking for them.

It is difficult to swim for nearly half an hour by yourself, let alone supporting a grown man with broken arms. Swansea and I both had to let the two of them go in order to save ourselves.

Half a day ago I would have been thrilled knowing I made it alive and ultimately saved the captain of the ship as well. But now all I could think of was how I couldn't save those two. The sailboat eventually approached, and my arms finally gave out as we were lifted to safety.

(II)

dormant like the rain

above it all
emotion brings weight that i do not wish for
perched to fall
following every movement

the more alone i remain
the longer i can stay

crowded
gathered
together
normal

(and i fall again)

as long as i am alone
i drift
the more alone i am
the higher i can be

i am not a tear
i am not the sea
i am not refreshing
nor can i be seen

emotion be gone
and let me stay
tendencies be gone
and let me be the rain

(III)

She looked just like Samantha Atwater.

I would never be myself again.

ALL HANDS

Everyone plays a part in the bigger picture.

(I)

Aboard the Pearson 424, Robert Garin Carlyle was content to be alive despite his dazed state of mind. He hadn't swallowed enough water to be sick, just thirsty, but it was not the fact he had to tread water for so long that had his head spinning. As he sat up and sipped from the cup of water brought to him, he couldn't help but stare at the redheaded beauty looking him and Swansea over. She had pulled men from wreckage before and considered his longing after her just that of a man saved from near-drowning. Hell, last time she was saved from wreckage she ended up ravaging her hero.

This was different though.

Robert and Swansea had not realized their own proximity until after their 3rd full cup of water. Curtis was busy maneuvering the ship through the wreckage so as not to be questioned. He was also struggling with how to conceal three extra persons instead of just the one he had when he awoke. Jones was past being a savior of others and was contemplating a name she should give these guys. Her real name was the safest, Cat, her middle name she never answered to, and her last name was a name that some sailors told stories about. The wind swept her red hair in front of her face chaotically and she gained control of it almost as quickly as she could the broken sails of a ship. She put her hair back, tying it off with a single strand of hair that she pulled from behind her left ear. There was a permanent wave to it as she was mainly in the humid air just above the ocean. On shore it would straighten out, but also gain thickness without the slight damp to weigh it down. As a true woman of the sea these were not her issues, just things she was aware of.

Even the way she put her hair back had Robert remembering playing hide-and-seek with Sam in their neighborhood. He considered introducing himself when he realized that the formality of names and introductions was something lost on the four people that were on this ship. He stood and walked past her, handing her his drinking cup with great thanks. She was impressed he could manage to walk without dizziness or evidence thereof.

"This your boat?" he asked her looking off towards the approaching shore.

"No, I'm just thankful to be aboard."

Swansea had been wanting to give thanks for the rescue but did not know just quite how. He took the opportunity, "Not as thankful as we are."

Cat Jones smiled and placed a focused eye on the old sailor, "You'd be surprised, my new friend, you'd be surprised." She began to stand up with Robert and poised herself inviting Swansea to join them. He took a deep breath contemplating his balance and declined the invitation with a firm exhale of current comfort.

Gaining his memory Robert felt familiar with the ship he now stood upon. This was the ship he saw stolen from the docks. This was the ship he walked upon in Dublin. There was really only one thing unfamiliar about the ship and it was her. However, in his life, she was most familiar. Only she wasn't Samantha Atwater.

Curtis came up from the cabin with a cup of coffee dangling from his mouth and three more encased between his two hands as best as he could. Cat was the first to hop over and help him out reaching for the one that seemed most uncomfortable steaming up into his face. Like a mother cat holding her newborn Curtis was not about to let it go. He mumbled with the cup tight between his teeth and his lips forming words as best as he could, "hmmmmhmmm, no. dishwansmine."

She smiled at the odd person that he was and pulled the center cup and one of the others he had better grips on. She kept one for herself and walked the short couple steps to the oldest member of the newly formed quartet.

Curtis used his free hand to grab the cup hanging from his teeth but instead of removing it immediately he pushed it up to grab a drink.

"First things first" Curtis said proudly swallowing his sweetened coffee as he reached the final cup out towards the man standing before him.

"Welcome aboard, Robert. I'm Curtis." The two men grasped hands tightly, knowingly, assuredly. They both knew of each other from the Liverpool dock and that would be the only time they openly acknowledged it. Swansea looked on to the moment as just another strange piece to this strange day. Cat Jones looked on to the moment as just another moment. The two men had a mutual understanding before that was cemented with their arrival on this ship.

"Alright, who's got a cigarette around here?" Swansea was unphased at how the men knew each other. He cut to the chase and decided he, too, could reunite with an old friend.

Jones piped up and offered to head down to the cabin to search the cupboards for him. He struggled to his feet, but found his balance, and made his way behind her to go help look. Shipwrecked, beat up, exhausted, there was always some energy remaining to find a cigarette. The old captain and the sea mistress went down to search through the stores of some rich man's lost items. Between the never touched flatware and the ornamental books with large print binding, Cat and Swansea both enjoyed the opportunity and excuse to peruse the belongings of someone else. They touched base on how Curtis didn't exactly own this ship, she let him know that she too had been rescued by this vessel, and he was loose-tongued enough she caught on to the fact he was partly responsible for the damaged cargo ship he didn't expect to get off of. They were fast friends, thick as thieves within a quick deconstruction of this cabin, and each found themselves diving into more details about their life than they would normally allow. Jones found an old cigarette pack and, making the assumption he was not particular at this point regarding expiration dates, chose to leave it partially hidden to continue her intrigue of this hardened man.

On deck the two men who had only known of each other were not so fast at gossip. They were getting to the point. Each could summarize the other well enough to know what they needed to know. Robert wasn't giving up much information but was open for action items moving forward. Curtis had an agenda and it was obvious to Robert. Curtis knew he was in no position to prove himself in Gibraltar arriving with anyone on board. They expected the boat to arrive with just the one man on it. It proved what they were looking for in experience. If they wanted to take the time to listen to how he found these shipmates, the story may actually go in his favor, but as far as they would be concerned a novice sailor, a woman, and an old man had to have boarded the ship when it set sail. Robert was quick to pick up on the dilemma at hand. He was aware the boat was stolen, hell, he was there to help the thief out and wish him farewell on his journey home. Robert wasn't exactly in a position to go against the flow with anyone and staying hidden from authority, official or not, was definitely a priority. He liked the idea of needing to stay away from being seen. The trouble was ensuring that only Curtis was seen on the boat. There was no way to tell if they would be waiting at the docks for the Pearson424 to arrive, or casually going to let Curtis settle in before announcing the boat had arrived.

Robert and Curtis both agreed to err on the side of caution and have the newly formed crew hidden from deck for the remainder of their journey. They could already see the shore and those awaiting Curtis were already on the lookout for the boat. It would be a roll of the dice. The three of them would simply stay out of sight, in the cabin, and wait for Curtis to find a way to keep it all under cover. There was a checkpoint of sorts that Curtis was supposed to find here. He hoped it was easy to navigate, however he also knew that Gibraltar was a big place and he was only told to show up. All signs pointed to him being expected and watched along the way.

All fine when there was only a crew of one.

(II)

They were on the western side of the Gibraltar Strait, mostly seen as the Spanish side, however this territory was actually part of the UK. Curtis knew he was being watched, but he didn't know at what point the observation would become detailed. Having not been given the exact position to land the Pearson in Gibraltar, he decided to forgo the main docks near the bay on this side of the peninsula, pass through the Strait of Gibraltar, and settle in somewhere on the eastern side with fewer residential areas.

Swansea and Jones had been through here before. It was a major sea alley connecting the Mediterranean and the Atlantic seas. Spain captured the majority of the northern lands from the shallow waters of the westernmost Camarinal Sill, up to the eastern most peninsula where the United Kingdom held onto the Rock of Gibraltar and the small bit of land around it. This was where Curtis would ultimately bring the Pearson to shore for his checkpoint en route to Egypt.

The currents below were massive, yet not so much noticeable at the sea's surface. The Mediterranean produced thick, warm salty water that pushed out into the Atlantic Ocean. It was so heavy that it virtually fell westerly into the Atlantic via the sea shelf created millennia ago when the two seas met for only the second time in their historic lifetimes after the Zanclean Flood. Current platonic movements predicted the enclosure again, but humans would not be around for this integration, at least not naturally. If enclosed again, the Mediterranean would dry up in a matter of a thousand years, regardless of temperatures rising or cooling at their estimated rates. More salt mines would come about than already exist, only then one could simply walk out to them rather than just being aware of their presence far beneath the water's surface.

The flow from one body of water to the next was enormous. The lighter waters from the Atlantic flowed quickly into the Mediterranean while the heavier saltier waters oozed along far below. The shallow waters where the Pearson was drifting over the Camarinal Sill, were lively areas of mixture. However, there was normally so much cancellation from eastern moving waters and western moving waters it was barely noticeable to sailing vessels.

German U-boats once upon a time cruised up into the deeper salt water unnoticed into the Mediterranean. Sixty-two total submarines approached without detection, however none of them would ever make their way back to the Atlantic.

At its narrowest point, the Strait of Gibraltar was merely nine miles wide separating two continents. Ferries traveled daily across allowing for easy transport and convenient movement. Wide enough for any cargo vessel to use it with ease and open to ultimately reach any major residential area of this hemisphere with products and supplies. The Spanish government laid claim to the Gibraltar lands where the United Kingdom held strong. They were beautiful lands providing entrance to often mystic lands, presented at one point in history as The Pillars of Hercules. So much power was naturally placed between these two land masses. The water movement here both provided and received from both directions. One side needed the other to perpetuate. At least on the scale of human needs.

This was a Mecca of movement, both natural and financial. Lives were built up because of the constant flow these waters had. Heavier, saltier waters below and the lighter waters of the Atlantic Ocean smoothly running into the smaller sea.

Below the surface was a powerful world that guided waters southwest towards the equator. Most importantly they moved the warm Gulf Stream Waters away from The North Atlantic Current and helped to sustain the frozen North. The strong currents and alternating temperatures guided sea creatures along their natural paths creating ecosystems that gave life to, not just the many coasts, but deep into the waters and the life that was held there.

The dense heavy water flow from out of the Mediterranean was as essential as the spoon in your coffee cup. It pulled the waters behind it, swirling around each side of the spoon, and not just blending the cooler waters and warmer waters, but disrupting the sugars and sediment at the bottom of your cup. Keeping things, temperatures and life, normalized. Especially in North America and Europe. There is a lot of power behind these waters, and a lot of influence would be had from a controlling party.

(III)

Above the surface the lighter and more agile Curtis stayed above to navigate the P424 past the Strait of Gibraltar and to keep up the appearance of a lone sailor onboard. Swansea, the thicker, saltier, and cooler sailor made his way down below. Robert and Jones had also stowed themselves below, not necessarily to help Curtis, but rather to hide themselves. At that point, both could have been considered dead at sea. Her because her identity was discovered and then the ship she was on blew up. Him because of the passport that would be discovered in the sinking cargo ship.

All four of them needed anonymity and all four would need each other to obtain it. Curtis for his stealth and sailing ability. Jones for her prowess and adaptability. Swansea for his connections and business sense. And Robert for his innate ability to observe and react, as well as his newly found passion to succeed.

In the cabin Robert took to the cooking duties and tried to find the right pieces to create a balanced meal. Pasta was plentiful. He had hoped for at least some salt and pepper and olive oil, but that wasn't happening as easily as he wished. Swansea lingered on the stairwell smoking his expired pack of cigarettes. Cat Jones alternated between the old books and exercise. It was tough to determine which was more relaxing for her. As she maneuvered her body into yoga positions, or through multiple series of pushups, she looked almost as though there wasn't a thought on her mind. Yet when she read she looked pained. Like there was truly a struggle to contain the knowledge she was pulling from the books. On the main deck Curtis cut the sails to slow the ship and find harbor closer to dusk than during the sunlight they were currently in. He rehearsed multiple conversations he thought he might have with people he had never met. None of the conversations would go the way he practiced, but it was what he could do to take his mind off the stowaways he'd picked up along the way.

Reports of the Pearson 424 being sighted in the area had already been made to those parties interested. However, those that spotted the vessel did not know the extent of what they were reporting and certainly did not know to scout for multiple sailors upon her. As far as they were concerned, this sailboat was in the wrong place amongst the shipping vessels that normally made their way through these waters and some parent was worried about an over privileged child that was given the keys to the Rolls for a weekend. It was also being observed that Curtis Scott was more inclined to hide amongst the shadows than in broad daylight. A lesson he would soon learn to change views on from the passengers on his boat. Although the sailboat did not match the description of most of the boats arriving on the western side of Gibraltar, it would not gather attention there. On the eastern side that Curtis was navigating towards, under the shadow of the massive rock formation, there were fewer non-native vessels and he would be seen as a tourist at best. The setting sun, especially with the dark shadow from the towering earth above the water's surface, would help to mask his flashy arrival in the P424.

Curtis found a public dock to pull in to. Being on a sporting vessel that did not usually cruise over such long distances, as well as having the confidence that he did, Curtis maneuvered into an area that was not looking to push the issue of customs and proper travel documents. Combined with the fact that those watching him were in charge of such things and would be intercepting him wherever he landed, his parking job would go virtually unnoticed. Their need for him to have a smooth interaction aided his anonymity arriving at Gibraltar. It was the southernmost dock along the east side of the mountain and it was used quite sparingly by the locals if ever at all. Its only access was through the mountain and Curtis had to navigate the tunnel and its stairs with a flashlight. He felt like the criminal he was. His best option was to avoid the shadows and attempt to be seen more lost than hidden. He exited the dock's tunnel near another tunnel. This one lead through the mountain to the other side and was built for vehicles, not pedestrians. He made the right decision and walked along the road on this side of the mountain crossing rows of condominiums and run-down hotels. No business seemed to be open for a long while. Being discovered soon turned out to be more difficult than he imagined. The locals here were not troubled by thieves or illegal immigration. The authorities, it seemed, would not be coming to him. He must find them.

It would be a long walk in a foreign country that would eventually get him where he wanted to be. An airport with a single runway crossing the peninsula from the west side to the east side was the closest to an authority he would find. Those on the commercial port side that had spotted the Pearson 424 had reported his presence in the area but had not found it terribly important to track him down. The local authorities had been alerted to be on the lookout for a man matching Curtis' description although they had not been told as to why. He was not to be considered dangerous, only a man of interest. The sailboat was left out of the description.

By the break of dawn Curtis had made it to the airport and managed to communicate that he was lost and needed to reach Irish authorities. It was not an outrageous request and one that had been quite expected. What he avoided was telling them where the boat was. He wanted to ensure his own safety, ability to travel home, and the money he was owed. He convinced himself that that order of things was his priority. It was in his best interest, and in theirs, to put any obligation to his stowaways far from a pressing concern whilst seeking his rewards. He sat quietly in a room with two men that he did not know at all and who barely knew why they were questioning him. Their lack of inquiry regarding the boat lead him to believe they were simply stalling until someone of greater authority arrived. This told him that there must be a series of notices running up a command chain and that soon his true employer would surface. These two grunts were just going through the motion of looking like they were higher paid than they actually were. They presumed he had arrived by plane and didn't think twice about asking how he arrived versus their persistence to find out why he was there in the first place.

Had they been working for his employer they would have known why he was there and would be far more interested in the whereabouts of the boat. Had they been his employer they would not have been worried about the boat at all, just the man before them. His ability was what this power truly needed. A resume was presented when this sailboat arrived at this harbor. This act of thievery combined with sailsmanship was symbolic of unconventional ability on the open sea. Not simply boatsmanship, where one can steer a vessel under motor, rather the ability to maneuver skillfully with the elements was what was needed. It committed an ability that went beyond the waters and winds of the ocean and suggested the control of the hearts and minds of men. Curtis had this skill and others wanted to prove it and exploit it.

The boat was both meaningful and meaningless. Its presence was worth ten times its own worth. Knowing it had arrived meant certain success for those that had requested it. Convincing a thief to fulfill their needs would not be so difficult. What was promised to Curtis would be paid. The contract would in fact be extended. The plans for his skills would take him to ports all around the Atlantic Ocean. The plans for his ability would create despair amongst countries that rely, perhaps too heavily, upon their imports and exports. The plans for his potential did not include the skills and abilities of those that were securing their trust below the deck of the very Pearson 424 that was the vessel to take them all to the next level. That boat housed both the rise and the fall of Curtis' new employer.

Curtis deflected the slightly better than amateur sleuthing the airport security officers presented for just over an hour. Their pride seemed to linger in the room like a foul odor after they were finally relieved of their stalling. Replacing them was one man. He had walked in and dismissed the two officers with a well-placed 'thank you' and an overwhelming amount of confidence. He sat with Curtis and placed two cups of coffee on the table moving one of the cups closer to the sailor.

"Four sugars" the clean-cut man said with just a hint of a British accent, "is that about right?" Curtis almost would have accepted a cup of black coffee this late in the morning. Almost. He accepted the cup of coffee without words. A simple nod and a first sip were enough to demonstrate that not only the proper amount of natural sweetener had been added to his beverage, but that the gentleman before him knew more about him than the average airport security guard.

Curtis had gone from feeling like he was being interrogated, poorly, to the feeling of being in a place of respect during a business meeting. The man never gave his name, rather he asked for the details of Curtis' trip. Curtis indulged him with simple heroism of the open sea. His stop outside of England, awakening from the slightest turns in the wind, and the large dolphin-like creatures he witnessed. He never mentioned the woman he saved. He never mentioned the old sea captain who survived a sinking cargo ship. And he certainly never mentioned the man who was somehow there when he acquired the ship and yet again right there with him when he brought the ship to its destination. He told the stories simply enough to avoid certain truths, yet the man he spoke to listened with great intent as if he had never ventured out to sea before himself. Knowing he had made the trip on a sailboat that could not have possibly carried enough gasoline to get here even if he had turned the motor on was enough to secure the continuation of the conversation.

As the cups of coffee made it back to their original empty state, the man presented a blank white envelope to the center of the table. "I'm authorized to give you this." Curtis graciously accepted the envelope folding it in half and shoving it into his back pocket. He had gathered that the man he was speaking to was not the one who was actually paying him for his task. This man had not even asked him to show him to the Pearson 424. He anticipated there being something more before this conversation was finished.

"There is more in that envelope than originally promised." Curtis had somehow expected that after seeing how inviting this conversation had been. He was ready to hear what else was expected as he knew it was not simply a gratuity added on to the bill. "We would like you to take the boat back out towards sea and head up to Lisbon. If you need gasoline, food, or any other supplies you'll have to stop along one of our docks on the western side of this little hill."

He had claimed a dock as their own. Curtis could not help but continually repeat that piece of the message over and over to himself committing it to memory. He told the man he was good with supplies and he smiled when he told him that the tank was nearly full. He made sure he asked for better direction for once he got in to Lisbon. Curtis wanted to remove some of the cloud of secrecy from the task this time and he was pleased to receive the direction.

"There is a large red bridge spanning Lisbon and Almada..." the man began.

"The April 25th bridge?" Curtis began with more ignorance than understanding of the area.

"Sure, Ponte Vente Cinco de Abril, or Ponte Salazar as the locals will call it. You'll make your way to the left, ugh... the Northern side, and dock there. You'll be looking for a white pier with red posts and many chalk designs. Find the British flag."

"Then that's when I get another envelope and the next riddle to solve sending me to yet another destination. Over and over again until back to Dublin I go?" Curtis could not help but imply his frustration with the secret arrangements.

"You'll hand the boat over to its new owner, Mr. Scott." He got to the point, "And from there I imagine you'll have enough money to buy a new boat or to fly yourself home."

(IV)

Robert sat on top of a stone wall watching cars and trucks disappear under the Rock of Gibraltar. The flow of traffic was nothing compared to that of the ocean's currents. This was completely random. He had better odds of predicting the color of the next car leaving the tunnel than how many would be in succession. Either way, he still liked the puzzle watching cars presented. It was somewhat peaceful testing his mind against something without a correct answer. He imagined this was what doing drugs felt like. Trying to decipher a riddle without an answer. Claiming to be on the verge of discovery only to get the wrong answer. Spinning another variable into the equation making the solution more and more improbable. Only he understood the complexity of what was before him. He would not fall victim to frustration and would simply marvel in its incredulousness.

She arrived quietly along the wall beside where he was sitting. It was what he had hoped for when he set out from the sailboat, but he had imagined she would sleep for a while. They had all three fallen asleep after Curtis made his way inland, but he had not slept for more than four hours before making his way up to watch traffic. Swansea would sleep longer this day than he had ever slept. He had no fixed obligations. This was the closest to a holiday he had ever had. He had always said someone would have to force him to stop working. It seemed this was the closest to exactly that that could have happened.

Her presence confused him. Not just here at the side of a road in Gibraltar, rather just her presence in the world. He tried very hard to find a physical difference between Cat Jones and Samantha Atwater. Samantha had avoided him for years and he only spent a day with her in Liverpool before she was taken from him. He was lost between a blurred memory and a woman who filled in the blanks that existed in the picture he carried in his mind. It was hard to decipher what was Samantha's likeness and what was hope. He did know that there was a great change inside of him around her. She gave him a chance to act like a new person. She gave him an opportunity to be someone that he wished Samantha had known. Cat gave him a reason to live and let go of his pursuit.

But she could not take away the fact that he was sought for murder.

They sat watching life on land as they had imagined it. There was no way to presume the fate of Curtis. He had given very little of his path away and he was just as likely to never come back for this boat as he was to come back with an army. Robert calculated that his own appearance was changed greatly enough by now, and imagined he was physically able to disappear into the land that was before him now. Only he did not have the means nor the knowhow to get the documents he needed to live in the modern world. He also wasn't quite fully committed to stop hunting for Samantha's true killer.

Cat Jones did have the means to acquire new passports, transportation and money. In fact, she still had plenty of money in the backpack she left onboard. Her issue was she really did not know where to go to hide away. She was still too well known despite her reputation leading most to believe she was a man. One day she would set out to fix that slight error. But for the time being it was safer to have those that wished her dead, and who possibly believed that she was otherwise, searching the world for a man who had been stealing from them.

There was a pressing connection between the two of them. It was clearly mutually beneficial, however neither of them knew exactly why and neither of them had the gall to bring it up to the other. He felt it ultimately came from the fact she looked like the woman that brought him to his present day. She felt it ultimately came from the fact he knew next to nothing about her and for her that meant a potential ally who did not default to thinking she would betray him.

Despite the lacking communication of their feelings, they would not hesitate to act upon the draw that was there. Jones and Carlyle, Cat and Robert, the past and the future of pirating along the Atlantic, sat wordlessly beside each other waiting for a man to return to take them towards their first adventure together. Curtis Scott was the key to everything they would need. They simply had to find the door and walk through it. It would seem easier before they reached the next step, but not until they realized how difficult the next step would be. As long as they both lived, the task ahead would always be stranger and more demanding than the last.

They remained silent not knowing what the next step would be. Robert thought the easiest route would be to follow this crew until he learned more about underground methods of acquiring things. Jones felt more comfortable out at sea, and especially not having to be in disguise or hiding away, yet she knew there was a large port not too far from here she could disappear into. If Curtis were not to return they did have the Pearson 424 at their mercy. It was being watched, however, and they knew it. To sail out on that ship without Curtis would lead to certain conflict. To sail out on that ship with Curtis would also lead to conflict. And to stay here and make their means without the ocean would invariably lead to conflict as well. They would wait and not push fate any faster than it needed to be pushed.

A taxi cab stopped a short way away from where they sat. There was a lookout point for those who wished to park their cars and watch the sea. Tourists and locals alike would pause to contemplate the vastness of the Mediterranean before them. Curtis got out of the back of the cab holding a bag from a local grocer. As the cab drove away Curtis looked up the road and spotted his crewmates sitting along the wall. He hopped up upon the short stone wall and turned towards the waves crashing upon the short shore. His observance was quick as he turned again to face the towering landmass to the west of him. He gazed upon its marvel as though he were witness to its slow movement over the course of time. He knew the waves behind him like an old friend. His curiosity was pressed in how such solid earth could be molded and shaped like a tidal wave waiting to crash and rejoin the waters from which it came. He turned back along the wall and skillfully walked the raised path to where Robert and Jones were sitting.

"Quite agile, Mr. Scott" Cat Jones said to him as he made it within earshot of the two of them.

He smirked at her compliment, "It's so much easier when the platform is not at the mercy of the water below. Are you two coming with? I'm headed to Lisbon."

Robert spoke for them both, "If you'll have us, we'd be honored to join you. Will we be stowed away beneath the deck again? Or are we free to move about this trip?" He only aimed to inquire directly, not imply anything beyond.

Curtis spoke directly to Robert after a quick glance at the woman beside him, "You know it's bad luck to have a woman on board?"

Robert was not too keen on sailor's superstitions, so he turned with a slight smile towards Jones. Her smile grew slightly greater than Robert's, "It's also quite lucky to have a cat on board, so I would think the two cancel each other out."

Robert suddenly felt he were watching a tennis match as he turned back to Curtis.

"Specifically, a *black* cat Ms. Jones. And we are travelling with two Jonahs whose last ship now sits at the bottom of the sea. So, either way, black cat or not, the odds are not in our favor. I may as well have brought a bunch of bananas before we set sail." He finished lifting up his small bag of groceries.

"You know it's unlucky to be superstitious." Robert added.

Cat and Curtis delayed their parrying and watched Robert as he hopped up and began towards the ship again. They followed and made their way to the Pearson 424 where Swansea was awake and waiting them.

"What's in the bag?" he asked Curtis as he stepped onto the deck.

"Don't worry, old man, he isn't brave enough to bring a bunch of bananas aboard" Cat taunted.

The old man didn't care for superstition, "That's too bad, I love bananas." He helped Cat aboard and continued, "So where are we headed? And are the stowaways staying aboard or forced to walk the plank?"

Robert chimed in, "We are headed to where your last ship was originally supposed to go... before we were met with fate."

"Lisbon." Swansea whispered noting that Robert never missed a detail.

"Yes" Curtis finally added, "We are headed to Lisbon. All aboard are welcome to stay aboard and I've got some coffee beans, sugar, oats, pasta, salt, pepper and razors... for those who need a shave. We... I" he corrected, "am expected there in three days."

Robert took his first step into a leadership role with this crew, "let's check that motor and get there sooner. It should be safer to go to shore that way. I believe Swansea may have some means for us to take advantage of once in Portugal." Swansea nodded with acknowledgment.

With the wind and sea against them north-bound along the Portuguese coast, using the motor was the best means. Even Curtis had to agree with that. He put on a pot of coffee and started the engine.

ABANDON SHIP

What matters now?

(I)

The Tagus River was ripe with sailboats out leisurely crossing below the red suspension bridge. The largest of its kind, trains and cars passed over the bridge while planes were capable of passing underneath. The weather had not been as pleasant for Curtis and his ship headed northward as it had coming down from Dublin. However, with the use of the boat's motor the strong winds and high waters just reminded him of how lucky he had been on the first leg of his trek. And despite the balmy overcast skies still present over the Tagus near Lisbon, there were a number of other sails raised over the boats that set out that day. Sailing in these waters had become a tradition that no lack of sunshine could overcome.

Robert stayed above deck as it was well before even 48 hours into their 72-hour expectation. Watching the movement of the boats along with the water was still mesmerizing. He felt he was getting better at noting its predictability. He even ventured to consider the bigger picture of how these large waters fed the even larger body of the Atlantic. He had now been south and north along these coasts. He had seen the Straits of Gibraltar into the Mediterranean. He was now at the mouth of the greatest river crossing on the Iberian Peninsula.

And he had done it all along the skill of a couple of the greats. His skills would only get better. It would all become a game to him just as the inner workings of computers had once become for him. There was a rhythm to all of it. And if you focused on the smallest wave you may feel there was less predictability there, but when you took a step or two back, or even a global approach, it all had a simplicity to it that was very mathematical and straight forward.

Cat, too, was above deck. In fact, Swansea was the only one who took full advantage of being able to stay below deck. Curtis of course stayed above watching the waters and, what was currently true, his ship. He enjoyed having Cat around. She unsurprisingly assisted him and naturally assisted correctly. She could predict what Curtis needed and he felt she was reading his mind. She, however, really only was doing what she was supposed to do and what came naturally to a skilled sailor. She was not actively trying to impress Curtis or read his mind, she was just sailing the only way she knew how.

Curtis went to Robert as he was more or less on lookout. The more or less just meaning there was no danger on the horizon; just he was already looking out at what was coming up upon them. They discussed the storms that had clearly passed here before they met with them along the way. The present humidity would seem to present a problem to their hosts and the welcome mat they were looking for. Chalk and water did not mix very well. Especially when the chalk they were seeking needed to be presented in the form of a British Flag. Piers with red posts were everywhere as the colors match the large red bridge they were underneath. Along one pier, however, Robert noticed some behavior that was unexpected. If this was a community that prided themselves on their chalk drawings over the piers, then why was there a stir of excitement from some children running along one of the piers? It seemed the joy in fact came from watching the chalk smear and run off into the water. This was the pier they were looking for and now they knew it. Only issue would be finding the area of the chalk washout that had the British flag.

Curtis was beside himself with confusion, "That's such a large deck to have so much invested into drawing upon it. Why on earth would they be excited about losing everything to a bit of rain? I bet the owners of the ships aren't so excited about it. I mean, I don't think I'd like to have to redraw everything. I don't even think I'd want to be required to have to paint my area in the first place."

Cat smiled, "If it weren't for the rain washing everything away how would you be able to start over again? Drawing on the deck is a sign of community, not a sign of following directives."

Robert smiled as he was instantly convinced she was right. Curtis looked bright-eyed back towards the dock and went to steer the vessel towards it.

He expertly brought the Pearson 424 upon the edge of the dock and let Cat and Robert jump off onto its sturdy form. Swansea came above deck to observe as he could feel the maneuvering of the boat and was ready to explore. Curtis moved out into a holding pattern while the two members of the crew walked the area. Along the pier were many children and a few adults walking with them as they admired the smear of colors draining into the waters under the pier. Cat's theory about a psychological restart must have been spot on as the two of them were greeted by smiles if they were even noticed at all by the locals enjoying the scene. At their feet were smudged caricatures of what must have been families, local folklore, and running jokes amongst the sailing community. Colors and shapes that once stood out boldly from one anther were now starting to fade and run together. However long it had been since a heavy rain washed the pier must have been too long. Shouts and giggles came from all over as children watched masterpieces distort and bend out of place like a multitude of circus mirrors in a fun house.

It was hard not to get caught up in the excitement. Even with the humid cloud cover the atmosphere was more like pure sunshine. Cat and Robert kept a lookout for the blue white and red of a British flag hoping it was not lost with the weather. Faded, but discernible, they found it finally and looked out for the Pearson. They found the ship and waved to Robert who made his way back to dock the ship in its requested position. The two land-dwellers kept moving along to not draw attention to the marked location and allowed Robert and Swansea to come aboard and join them.

As the sun later came out and cut the humid air, Cat made her way back to the ship to find her bag. The three stowaways were set on finding a cottage or hotel and to post up for the night. Curtis only requested the use of a shower to avoid the difficulties of the onboard shower that were only a luxury when there was no alternative. He would still make his residence onboard that evening as he never knew exactly when he would be meeting up with another envelope.

(II)

Many from the town of Lisbon joined the sailing community based more on their artistic skills rather than their innate ability to avoid seasickness. Drawing upon the docks had long been a tradition that nobody seemed to know the full history of. Whether it was a community coming together to bond in ceremony or a claim to individual territory along the valuable waterside of the city, it had blossomed into a tradition of creativity and togetherness. During the summertime when there were larger windows of time between the rainfalls, the designs would flourish with details and artistry.

During the fall the locals would come and vote upon their favorites over the summer by collecting around them and simply holding their conversations while standing on top of them. The foot traffic about the caked-on chalk would begin the process of loosening the drawings and erasing them. The more popular drawings were worn into the souls of everyone's shoes and taken away by the masses. An artist's sense of pride was truly enhanced when their artwork was taken away instead of left behind.

The designs that remained were washed away by the power washers coming through and bringing the docks back to their wooden normalcy. Those from Lisbon that had a permanent place at the pier, yet stowed their sailboats elsewhere during the winter, left their marks like family crests upon the tough wood. Through the lesser visited times of the winter these markings held like acorns underground marking the spot for next spring's great oaks.

Spring would finally come, and festivals were held to mark the coming of the open sailing seasons. Children would decorate, and families would gather to watch the chalk creations as well as see the majestic sailboats reunite with the Tagus River. The multitude of showers during this season allowed for many opportunities for the chalk drawings to be washed away and leave fresh canvases for new creations.

This summer had been particularly daunting, and the sun was winning the battle of the skies over any storm clouds. As the spring festivals were heavy with sailboats, the chalk drawings lasted longer and were not needed to be replaced as often as the many children of the city would have enjoyed. The fast-moving storm that threatened to remove the British flag marking the Pearson's landing point had been well received this time during an unusually hot summer. Many would turn out to decorate the public spaces of the docks and many would arrive early to rope off what they could to demonstrate their mastery of the chalk medium. Before the early morning sun reared its heat above the horizon, teams made their ways to clear the pier and ready the canvas for the day's endeavors. Many found this to be an unmarked holiday and would take full advantage of the occasion.

Curtis worried that it would make it more difficult to find his connection. Robert and Swansea found no difference between this overcrowded dock and the exact opposite. Cat found the opportunity to blend in with such a crowd that she could not possibly be noticed. She reveled in the ability to be completely anonymous. Somehow it only happened when she was on land.

She wandered between the locals as they began to gather around the waterways. Swansea and Robert made their way farther inland to settle into a café and Curtis went hunting along the wayside to find a street vendor and grab a quick bite. Cat found him on his travels back to the ship and invited herself to join him.

"You look nervous." She said delicately trying to avoid any misinterpretation.

"Land makes me nervous." He told her as they walked through the crowds. "Land and traveling half-way down the globe to sell a stolen ship to someone I've never met. Those two things."

She smiled, "Just those two things, huh? Not storms or guns or taxes..."

"No, storms I've never really had control over, haven't really been shot at enough to learn to worry about guns... and taxes, well, I've never had an actual income to have to worry about taxes. So, yeah, just selling this boat."

"And land." She added.

"Mostly land." He acknowledged.

Back at the ship they went down below, and he started a pot of coffee out of habit. She wondered if it was the last time she would be in the Pearson or if they would be sent off on another errand. She grabbed her backpack just in case.

"Taking off?" Curtis hoped for a no but fretted a yes.

"Just in case, y'know?"

"Yeah, I get it." He tried not to think about her as more than a comrade; however, it was just too much. He was not normally one to get caught up in his emotions, especially over women, but she was something else. She outmatched him in every way that mattered to him. Sailsmanship, stoicism, espionage...being alone. He longed for a companion that was more independent than he. Only he never imagined he'd fine her. And he'd never imagined that whoever she was would not fall head over heels in love with him. Somehow that had just made the most sense to him.

They talked about possible next steps while the coffee brewed. Never did they feel they were planning the future, just discussing 'what-ifs'. Halfway through her first cup of coffee, and during his third, they made their way to the bow of the ship to watch the activities about the port. Neither of them saw the flow of the crowd the way that Robert would have. They did not see the unity of the masses nor were they able to predict the flow based on events within the sea of people. Curtis and Cat watched each person as they did their own boat. They watched small groups of people like they did the waves that were immediately upon them at sea. They each smiled when they saw someone laugh at a friend's joke. Both of them could sense the joy of a parent watching their children talk about the drawings they'd made. They never once watched a sequence of events and considered how to change, correct or manipulate any of it.

The two men walking through the crowd towards them went unnoticed until they were too close to scramble. Not that they needed to, Cat being there was not really a concern, but it was too late to even consider movement. One had an oversized backpack on and each of them carried briefcases.

Curtis rose from his elbows anticipating their arrival starboard. Cat waited until he had invited them aboard before she went to him, grabbed one of his hands and leaned in to kiss him on his cheek. She nodded politely to the two men and stepped off the boat. The two men followed Curtis down below deck and Cat made her way to get lost in the crowd again.

(III)

Robert gathered the food order he had placed for himself and Swansea and made out into the dining area to find his companion. The diner was busier than usual with the previous night's rains providing a fresh start for artistry today and the staff had not been bumped up properly to accommodate. He found some joy there. He was far from too impatient to be worried about a 2-minute coffee or a 6 minute coffee and enjoyed the thought of witnessing the moment that might be making someone stronger in their future endeavors. His stroll through the dining area took a little longer than it should have, but he was in no hurry and Swansea wasn't one to pay attention to the details when he wasn't the one in charge.

He finally found the old captain on the popular patio sitting at the smallest table there. He brought the vittles over to the table and sat down.

"I wasn't exactly sure if black coffee was your thing or if was just what you'd been drinking the past couple weeks." Robert said trying to suggest casual conversation.

Swansea stared off pre-focused on something, or someone, much more causative of his attention than the coffee before him.

"See that guy?"

Robert turned mildly away, "You'll have to be more specific." He looked back to Swansea, "a lot more specific."

"There's a guy at the corner table, wearing clothes too warm for today like it was unexpected, who cannot stop staring at the pier."

Robert spotted him, "The one fidgeting with his coffee and his phone wishing one or both was a stronger drink?"

"Exactly." Swansea got up, "I know him."

Robert did not get the feeling that these two were best of friends. It wasn't exactly something that felt concerning, but Swansea's demeanor certainly made him feel that this guy should not have been where he was. Hell, none of them really should have been where they were that day. He grabbed his coffee and hoped that Swansea would make it back before he had to start drinking his.

The man was gigantic. He looked a bit too large for his own control and seemed like he had just accepted his awkwardness throughout life. He recognized Swansea immediately and looked to lose his focus for just a moment. He certainly looked uncomfortable when Swansea sat at his table to talk to him. The old man was not one to just strike up a conversation with anyone so there must have been a focused dialogue, but the stranger seemed overly occupied with the pier now that he had been recognized. The only time he stopped looking at the docks was to glance at Swansea, except the one time he took a deliberate effort to look back at Robert and evaluate the situation. Robert knew he stuck out like a rubber raft at the docks sitting in that foreign land, but he didn't feel out of place enough to worry that the man was drawing any conclusions beyond having recognized him as Swansea's breakfast companion.

The oaf punched at his phone with more intensity than Swansea could withstand watching and he finally got up and began his trek back to Robert and his breakfast. He was sitting down to rejoin Robert, "That guy manages the docks in Dublin. I thought he'd be the perfect person to get us out of here, but I couldn't figure out what he was doing here."

Swansea began shaking his head with perplexity when an explosion burst out from the docks. The sound was deafening, and the ground shook below them. Tables overturned, drinks spilled and wood from the docks slammed into the sides of buildings. Ships were tossed out into the river and others up onto the shore. People and families were torn apart killing many instantly and, for others less fortunate, injuring them terribly. Before the fires could erupt into thick black smoke and the screaming began, three figures rose on the deck of the small diner.

Bradly O'Sheel looked out onto the chaos scanning the scene as it moved from slow motion into a real-time disaster.

Swansea looked about the deck to see if he could help anyone near him.

Robert Carlyle looked only towards Bradly O'Sheel. The man seemed certain to have known something about this and there was a confidence about the situation that put the Pearson 424 right in the midst of things. He noticed Bradly take a hesitant step towards the disaster which told him he was either not very aware of his own actions or he was not exactly expecting the situation to unfold this way. Either way, he did not look as if he knew what to do next. Robert took strides towards the man hoping to find out what he did know. Swansea knelt near a couple who had both taken some damage from flying pieces of the dock. Neither was in life threatening danger, but the woman was beginning to cry from the realization of what happened, and her companion was showing the first signs of entering into shock.

"Hold here. Lots of pressure, do you understand?" He told the man who only could listen and follow orders at this point. "Do not let go until help comes to you. And realize that whenever help arrives, there are others that they will go to first." The man nodded as Swansea stood and started to follow Robert.

"Lots of pressure!" he hollered back towards the man who may or may not have been able to hear anything at that point.

Robert pulled the back of Brad's shirt down bringing him reluctantly back into his chair and sat next to him.

"You obviously know something about this." He began his interrogation, "What do you know?"

"This wasn't supposed to happen. Not now."

"So, you did know there would be an explosion."

Swansea walked up just in time to hear Robert's confirmation, "You did this?"

Bradly turned towards him, "Not like this. Not now. This changes… this changes. This changes something. I don't know."

"How was it supposed to go? You trying to kill Curtis?"

"NO!" Bradly stated assuredly. "No way. And you don't know he's dead."

"He was on that boat, Brad. Did you put a bomb on there?" Swansea jumped right into a 'Bad-cop Bad-cop' routine forgoing the alternative.

"The men I sent to talk to Curtis where supposed to plant a bomb, yes, but not set it." He began to gather his wits about him and overcome his shock from this predicament.

Robert started in again to try and solve the problem, "What was supposed to happen when you planted a bomb on a boat in a crowded deck if this was not the intended result!?"

Bradly looked at him and regained his sense of entitlement and authority. He looked at Swansea and back out at the mess that was unfolding on the beach before them. "Let's see what we can find." He got up and did not stop the others from joining him. In fact, he hoped for it and got what he wished.

It was a calamity that happened all too quickly and caused great damage and certain loss of life. Truly a disaster was unfolding right before them. All three men blamed themselves one way or another.

The sheer silence following the explosion was not noticeable until the screaming began. Those with the least amount of physical injury were the first amongst those that cried out in emotional pain. The sight of those with severe injury was hard to take.

Bradly, Swansea and Robert follow a trail of broken limbs and gashes that thickened the closer to their destination they got. The docks were nothing but floating burning lumber and mix and match boat pieces. No one shouted for help. Those that could muster up the lung capacity to yell only cried out for specific names. The names were as unrecognizable as the faces from which they came.

Not even a full minute had passed since the bomb went off yet it had felt like a lifetime. For some it had been.

People far enough away to not be impacted and close enough to help began their approach. Slowly the balance of the well grew to match that of the hurt.

Robert looked down at the chaos, "I don't know how you could find anyone in this mess."

Swansea rebutted, "There are many to find if you're not particular about it, Robert."

Bradly heard none of their philosophy, "I see some people swimming in from out in the river. I think they were lobbed outwards." He looked at the men, "Perhaps he is one of those."

Robert looked away out towards those he was talking about, "If he is out there, and he's alive, he'll be bringing others in with him."

"Aye, now that's a fact." Swansea added.

Bradly added on, "let's move out, if we can, and see who we can bring in. Help will be here shortly for those on the land." He said so as if he already knew that help were on their way. And they were. They just weren't expecting to be needed quite as early as this.

Nearing absolute exhaustion Curtis Scott turned a man on his side in hopes that if he did cough up water it would not be cause to drown a second time. He went back into the river to seek anyone else that could possibly be there. The cuts through the bottoms of his feet would not be noticed for at least another trek out and back.

It was the man he had brought to shore that caught the attention of Bradly, Swansea and Robert. He lay too perfectly near the edge of the water to have landed there and he did not look like he was capable of having swam there himself. Somehow Curtis had made it off the boat and had been flung into the waters.

Had they been looking closer on their walk they would have seen a group of children being comforted by a kneeling woman who at a glance looked like one of them.

Cat Jones must have had yet another life to spare.

(IV)

Curtis had been on the deck of the Pearson after the two men demanded privacy to inspect their employer's purchase. They never had the opportunity to question him or provide him the next steps of his strange journey. He was to meet with Bradly that day but under the veil of celebration, not tragedy. Launched out from the explosion into the waters Curtis would barely remember the depth he plunged below the surface of the Tagus. Floating upwards to the surface was more of a dream, however the rush of oxygen into his lungs breaching above the waves would be an awakening he would never forget.

The soles of his feet would need surgical repair as they had been cut open in several places. Bradly would see to it that he received the care he needed as he controlled police, fire and rescue along most coastlines and in many major ports. This was not the reunion he sought after with his friend.

Curtis managed to bring a second lifeless body to the shores before he fell victim to exhaustion and collapsed half way on solid ground. Swansea had seen him first and called out to Robert. It was still Bradly that got to him first. Emergency crew arrived on the scene much quicker than normal response time despite the premature detonation of the bomb. No one would ever take the time to have calculated that or ever learn the reasons why they happened to be ready nearby.

With Curtis secure Robert began scanning the faces along the broken shoreline for Cat Jones. She had already found him and his new companion from her standing position within the crowd. She watched only long enough to confirm who the man was when he lifted Curtis and turned to carry him to safety.

Robert finally saw her as she paused, calculated and turned away. He wondered how he would ever be able to contact her again as she disappeared into the city. He turned back towards Bradly O'Sheel and wondered who this man was that Swansea knew, nearly killed Curtis, and had Cat turning back towards land to fall into her familiar world of shadows.

He would not let him get too far from his side.

HOGMANAY

Preparing for the end.

(I)

His height and weight did not prevent him from being thrown around. With the right leverage, positioning and quickness, Brady O'Sheel's red locks slammed against the mat white paint on the hospital wall. Robert's shaggy locks flying forward into his own face.

"What the fuck" he choked audibly. His eyes rolled up just as his hands when they grasped at the stronghold around his neck.

"Why the fuck did you attack Curtis?" Robert was even shorter than Bradly now that he had him pinned up against the wall, but he certainly acted much taller in this moment.

"It makes zero sense." He said quietly, almost to himself, while the pressure kept Bradly from ever addressing the question.

Swansea hustled towards the two but had no intention of interfering. He didn't really know Robert that well, and certainly didn't know what he was capable of. He was learning in this moment he was quite capable of handling himself against a much bigger opponent. Swansea had seen Robert in action before, but there was also an explosion happening behind him and the threat of drowning forcing some adrenaline. This was pure emotion.

A nurse saw the event and started to rush to the scene.

150

Bradly, despite his lack of ability to speak, raised an arm towards her and waived her away. He was in this business – the intimidation business – and fully understood what the situation was and what he needed to do. Besides, it wasn't the first time someone put him in a choke hold.

The nurse hesitated and slowly walked backwards. Robert, taking the right cues, softened his grip and let Bradly get some air.

It wasn't a pretty situation, and there was a lot the Bradly had to tiptoe around with these guys, but he also felt there was a lot he could gain with men like the ones Curtis was now acquainted with.

His feet now firmly on the ground he rubbed his throat, "I understand why you're frustrated. I love Curtis, too. More than you could ever know." Robert wasn't quite sure he loved Curtis, but now wasn't the time to sort the difference between respecting a human being and protecting a friend's honor. Bradly continue, "Never. Never! did I mean to hurt him." He stepped forward and established a better balance of control between him and Robert. He was clever enough not to overstep. He knew Robert needed control right now and he understood why. He was also comfortable navigating the situation, sharing information, and coming to a common conclusion with the man in front of him.

"Can we take this outside?" Bradly proposed to Robert.

Robert stood stoic.

"The conversation... not the incident." Bradly defined. "The conversation implied by all of this. Let's have it."

Robert hadn't seen such control over a heated moment before. Up until everything in his life went in this direction, he'd never really been in a fight. And although he felt he'd grown pretty used to brute strength recently, he admired how easily Bradly diffused the situation and accepted his side of it. They made their way past Swansea and the hospital waiting room and down a long empty, very sterile, hallway to talk it out.

There clearly were certain styles he could pick up from Bradly. And if he could use this relationship to his advantage, he could learn more about who this guy was, what was happening, and hopefully what started him on this strange journey.

"Look" Bradly began slowly, "I don't expect anyone to ever forgive what happened to Curtis. Least of all me. But I know for a fact that it was an accident. It was not supposed to happen when it happened. Only the boat was supposed to be destroyed and we were going to make sure there was nobody on that who would have been seriously harmed."

"Then what happened?" Robert believed him, still didn't like it or understand it all, but he believed the big man. "How did it get out of your control?"

"No idea. They must have triggered the explosion. Simple as that."

"Okay, so the bigger question. Why?"

"Well we didn't need the boat anymore, that's obvious. And it was a way for me to free Curtis up for some more hidden work."

Robert listened to the concept and realized Bradly was opening up some insight to a bigger picture. "So, he'd go into hiding, but now with this injury he's out in the open, huh?"

"Yeah it's fucked up in a number of ways. Mostly with my friend. But, yeah, to your point now this is very public and everyone who wants to know if he's alive knows."

"So, you were supposed to kill him." Robert stated boldly. "Like, what, some sign of loyalty that you were willing to take out your best friend?" Bradly's look confirmed it without comment.

"Has this worked before?"

"Haven't tried it, to be honest." Bradly continued, happy to be moving on with the conversation. "But we've seen it a few times now from a thief who has damn near exploited us over and over again."

"Whoever he is clearly has pissed you off in addition to whatever has been stolen."

"She." Bradly corrected. "Everyone else thinks Jones is a man, but I've seen her."

Robert couldn't believe what he was hearing. It was too much of a coincidence and Cat was… shit, was she? She did slip away as soon as she saw Bradly at the scene.

Bradly was too occupied to notice that Robert was lost in his thoughts beyond the conversation at hand. He couldn't believe the crossroads being presented to him.

"What's she trying to steal?" Robert collected himself and thought he'd start digging for something bigger. There was too much here. Too much coincidence. Cat. Samantha. Deception. Attempted murder. Sabotage. Cover up. Too much.

"Mostly cash at this point." He concluded. "But she's disrupting everything we're working towards. And if she has the right info, and the right people, she could shut this whole thing down."

"She wouldn't just shut it down, Bradly. You'd be in jail. You and… whoever." Robert couldn't believe what was being shared with him. He wasn't going to question it, he was going to push. Push until he tied it together or ruled it out.

"Well…" Was all Bradly could muster.

"They'd have you take the fall, huh?" Robert asked knowingly. "I've got an idea so that we could minimize the eyes watching over the whole thing." He saw his opportunity.

"I'm listening"

"Swansea is on the level, and he's really fucking good at what he does. We put him in charge of loading several shipments throughout the weeks here in Lisbon." Not himself, he was new to all of this.

Swansea! Yes! Swansea was already in, knew what he was doing and could buy Robert time to figure things out.

And it would keep the focus off of him. He had no idea what authorities were still looking for him.

Bradly thought about it, "No, I need him to captain a ship."

"He'd captain all of them. That's the point." Robert had a determined look on his face like he'd solved a great mystery and needed to lay out the details, "Your men unload the ships, right?"

Bradly acknowledged him.

He was thankful his suggestions were finding solid ground.

"And it's not like your 'captain' is really inspecting cargo when they load the ships"

"That's why we pay them... to *not* do their job."

"Yeah," Robert continued, "and I've been on the ship with Swansea. It's not like he needs to be there to navigate to port. His men don't rely on him to do their job. He sets it up and it sails..."

Bradly was catching on, "So you're saying he's the 'faux-captain' for every ship leaving this harbor?"

"Why not? Who's validating it?"

"I am."

"And how much would you save and how much more confidence would you have in the 'captains' you'd have to pay off?"

(II)

Curtis had suffered numerous cuts and bruises, but none more serious than the large lacerations on his feet. His pain was so tremendous that when he was awake he was pumped full of pain medication. He was never focused enough to ask anyone what had happened and only described the Pearson and his journey within it. It was as if that boat had become a part of him; comforting him during his time of unrest. When he was awake he only looked for Cat but never saw her by his side. He never asked where she was. He remembered the wreckage and if she had fallen with it he did not want to know. His confusion over seeing Bradly did not steer him towards the trusted childhood friend. And, in fact, he could not figure out how Robert and Swansea suddenly appeared by his side. He would wait and learn when he had his wits about him better.

For now, he would sleep.

(III)

Cat Jones had to rummage through her backpack for the first time in a matter of weeks. She hadn't dared to open it although she felt she could have trusted her previous shipmates. Pushing bundles of cash aside she grabbed some clothes that would be a bit more fitting for life on land. In fact, it was really the only outfit she had in the bag.

Pulling from a roll of bills, she managed to secure a hotel room a bit inland from the pier. She felt the farther from her life at sea she could physically get the less likely she was to be recognized. Her first morning alone she went to three different coffee shops and purchased a single cup of coffee with a large bill so that she could begin to buy things without only using such obvious money. Having three consecutive cups of unnecessary coffee reminded her of being with Curtis on the Pearson. She had been on many ships and sailed as a passenger and as a sailor with many others. Yet the three of them on that ship struck her with a strange emotion. She'd felt at home. Relaxed for the first time in forever. There was a connection there she could not quite understand.

Yet the sight of Bradly O'Sheel struck her with another emotion altogether. She was either scared or relieved. Either he was on to her, or he wasn't that good at what he was out to do. Either she was on to something or he was. She recognized him by rumor alone. He was the one that was after her. Her profit over the last few years were proportional to his losses. Especially the job that ensured her backpack was currently filled with cash. O'Sheel wanted her dead. There was a bounty on her head and there were stories about attempts and close calls. Cat knew that there never had actually been a close call, she wouldn't allow it.

And sometime last year she caught wind of her own death from her sources in England. Apparently, she'd been taken out by some hitmen while walking through a park. Hearing that she stayed away from parks more often than she had already.

Not too many parks out in the open sea.

And no matter the number of parks she could find while in Lisbon, she kept to the metro. The more public the area the better. Making herself comfortable in the middle of town, she had a quick route to the airport or the seaport. Although she kept away from both. It was just nice knowing the options were there in case.

The first week in Lisbon she stayed at a hotel. Learning the streets, the back streets, and getting a feel for how the city flowed. There was always a life within the city that was intimate for those that took the time. Any city. Every city. And if you didn't take the time to get to know it, you would forever be a foreigner. Or worse, a tourist. Cat Jones couldn't afford that risk. She felt comfortable that Swansea and Robert didn't mention anything to Bradly about her. If they had she certainly would have felt the heat. Or met someone who would confirm the suspicion. And she knew that whoever that would be wouldn't be mentioning the fact that someone was after her, it would indeed be the very person who was after her.

She hoped Curtis was alive to know she was gone. She couldn't decide if she'd rather know he was alive and that he had spoken her name, or if it were better he were gone and kept silent. She wasn't one to put the hope out there in terms of exactly what she wanted: Curtis alive and not talking. In fact, Curtis alive and talking to her would be best, but it wasn't time to confirm that just yet. She was far from deciding when that time would be.

The Lisbon Metro was sufficient enough to get around town. She shopped for clothing and made herself comfortable. There was value and risk in getting into a routine, but she began to become complacent that her location was safe. She dug into Lisbon for some time.

After a stay at a second hotel she managed to find a room to stay in. She had become a regular at a few coffee shops. Some were strictly for coffee, some were for breakfast and others for lunches. She had a favorite for getting online and searching the net, but she didn't know what she was looking for. Any information about the bombing at the docks was limited. Obviously, it was an inside job. At least it was obvious to her. She knew who did it and knew he was as inside as inside gets.

Cat had warmed up to a barista name Olvidio. He was quick to recommend a bite to eat and seemed to know when she just wanted to have coffee and be left alone. She admired that he knew his trade so well but was astonished when she learned of his love for the outdoors. He was not a sailor, so she was in no threat of having to act like an amateur, rather he was a climber. She didn't spend enough time on land to know that people took the time to seek a more difficult route to the top of something that might have had stairs. But he traveled often enough, was set in his own agenda and had a spare room that kept her off the beaten path. She kept to herself often but was never anti-social. Whenever Olvidio was home she would visit with him and allow him to tell his tales of climbing and the terrors of customer service. His thick Spanish accent was fun for her. She was used to the thick abrasive accents of sailors that were more likely to offend than inspire.

He was sensitive and sweet, focused on fitness and self-exploration as he pushed his body to its physical limit. He was the exact perfect man for her to be around and never gain interest in. Olvidio enjoyed Cat as she was always willing to listen to his stories no matter how much exaggeration he added. He was easy going and she was always on time with the low rent he had requested from her. And he always called her Catrina, which she adored.

She had disappeared before yet somehow this time she felt she was truly gone. As though she had lost the sea and found a new person. She was never naïve to her true place in the world, but for now this was the right place to be in.

From here she could see everything.

(IV)

Swansea was in a strange position sitting with Bradly O'Sheel and Robert Carlyle. He had always been the one that people knew the least about. Now he sat with a man he knew accepted less than the going rate for work under the table, and another man who had his fingers deeper into the world's ports than he'd ever imagined someone could. He was just a simple cargo ship captain that occasional made the illegal haul for extra cash. Now the underground world of moving oil seemed petty to him, and that was okay.

The three maintained this facade while Curtis healed. At first there was awkward tip-toeing around the bomb explosion at the docks, but Bradly wasn't letting on to any better details. At least not publicly since Robert and he had their discussion. Bradly also knew to keep these two close even with the limited understanding they had of the situation. In fact, he recognized how fortuitous the current situation was for his bigger plan. His attempt to force Curtis into his services quickly gave him three for the price of one.

Robert hadn't expected Bradly to give up much ground regarding the incident at the docks. He understood that not sweating any more details than he had would prove beneficial to his own ultimate goal. Bradly was obviously a man with connections beyond the law and Robert needed to get up above it somehow. He also knew that Cat Jones recognized him immediately and vanished, and that Bradly would have recognized her if he had the chance.

Neither he nor Swansea had mentioned their stealthy companion. His only concern there was if Curtis said something before they could align with him then Bradly might lose what little trust had been developed.

Swansea was hesitant at first to take on the extra chore of multiple vessels. He didn't dare ask for more money, but he went about the plan as Robert had explained to him. He didn't even mind that Robert seemed to be taking a stronger role in this whole thing. In fact, he was pretty okay with it.

Instead of checking in one vessel and taking her to the next port, he went about his routine with the cargo, the men on board and even the navigation. He did everything to the letter up until it was time to take off. Then he just left the boat and did it again for the next.

He didn't know how it wasn't being noticed. And, frankly, he didn't care. He didn't want to know. All he knew was that instead of faking spot-checks on deck once a week, now he was doing it several times a day. He still didn't know what was in the containers exactly, and he planned on keeping it that way.

Not everyone shared that perspective.

One rainy morning Swansea was out performing his new routine.

"That seems to all be in order." He reiterated to a member of the crew on board, "You have the route? Can you handle navigation from here?"

"Aye, Captain. Nothing we haven't done before."

Swansea muttered something under his smoky voice and stepped away from the quarters. The rain threatened to put out his light and his cigarette, but he'd get the job done. He always did.

It didn't matter that the rain had kept the morning darker than usual, blotting out the sun was far easier than preventing this old seaman from pulling his love of tobacco deeper into his lungs.

As he stepped down the ramp and back towards the dock, leaving the ship he was still on according to all records, he looked over at the port's crew preparing for this ship to leave and the next to be loaded. Everything seemed in order.

"Hello old friend."

Two stunning green eyes somehow found light in the darkness and peered nearly through him. He dropped his cigarette and didn't even realize it.

"It's not like you to stop smoking for anyone, but I appreciate the gesture." Cat Jones prowled closer to him and right past him looking up at the boat he just exited.

"Cat?"

"How many ships are you setting off on today, Swansea?"

"I…" he hadn't the words. How did she know?

She ran her hand down his arm, dripping wet from the rain. Unknown words were buried even further in his mind.

"How much do you know?"

"Only what I need to."

"How much will you tell me?" She paused to gauge his reaction.

"As much as I can." He answered truthfully. She believed him. She also recognized he was smart enough not to learn more than he needed to.

"Bradly is a bad man. He does awful things for awful reasons." He heard her. "I don't suppose you know why he's doing all of this, do you?"

"Money?" the old man attempted.

"Don't guess, my friend." She let go of his arm slowly, "He has enough money already. There's something else going on. They already control the ports… you know that, right?"

Swansea nodded thinking that much was obvious.

"They're tracking the weather. The wind and the waves." She watched him to see if he might know anything about that. He didn't. "But 'why?' is the question."

"I don't know."

"We will." She assured him as she started to walk away, "No need to keep this a secret. You let them know I'm around."

Cat walked off into the rain and Swansea instinctively reached for another cigarette.

(III)

He walked along the beach looking upwards towards a single star that shone brighter than any he had ever seen before. It was perhaps the most beautiful thing he had ever seen. The mountain nearby seemed to be tall enough to reach it and he wondered what it would take to have that star as his own.

A beach dweller sat by his campfire watching the shimmer from the starlight over the water in front of his camp.

He walked towards the man seated cross-legged by his fire still while looking up and marveling at the sight above him. "I wish I could touch that star" he said not knowing if the man could even hear him.

"I'm not the one that can grant your wish, my friend." The long pause that followed was mutual as it felt the beach dweller had not yet completed his thought. "You must share your dream with that mountain and follow the path to where you can find your wishes come true."

He looked back towards the mountain and saw a thin trail that winded up and around a small pass. The seated man never looked away from his fire and he was somehow inspired by the heavy knowledge that had been passed to him.

He walked to the path and followed it upwards. He finally came to an open area where he saw an altar that overlooked the ocean. This must be the place that will grant my wish. He gazed up again at the star above he so longed to be with. At the altar he spoke, "I wish I could touch that star."

A voice came to him as he waited, "This altar cannot grant your wish, my friend. You must share your dream with the mountain and follow the path to where you can find your wishes come true."

And there again the man saw a thin path running farther up the mountain side. He looked up upon the star and smiled longing to reach out and touch it. He accepted the path before him and began to climb again until he reached another opening and another altar. This must be the altar I can wish upon, he thought, and he looked up again at the star feeling his wish would bring him near it soon.

"I wish I could touch that star." He said again to the altar as he watched the star's reflection on the water far below him. Again, nothing happened until he heard the voice.

"This altar cannot grant your wish, my friend. You must share your dream with the mountain and follow the path to where you can find your wishes come true."

He looked out for the path he knew now to look for. He found it much easier this time and with a look up at the star he wished for he readily made way to climb again. The star became more beautiful the higher he was on the mountain and his desire to reach out and touch it grew as big and bright as the star with every step he took closer and closer to it.

161

He came across another clearing and another altar. He walked happily towards the altar and first looked out towards the now distant sea below. He did not rush as he considered his words and believed them more and more before he spoke.

"I wish I could touch that star."

The voice again shared the same advice it had before, "This altar cannot grant your wish, my friend. You must share your dream with the mountain and follow the path to where you can find your wishes come true."

He was not disappointed at all and had already sought out the next path before the voice finished. Upon the end of that trail he would find another opening and another altar overlooking the sea. The star he so wished to be near looked down upon him and he up at it. He felt good about the next altar and that his wish would finally be granted.

Yet again the same thing happened upon the next altar. And again and again he climbed upwards seeking the altar that he could finally wish upon and have his wish come true. Every time the voice would answer his wish to touch the star with the same advice about sharing that wish with the mountain and continuing upon the path.

Until finally the man came to a clearing and he looked out for an altar and one was not there. He looked up towards the star he longed for and with his heart pounding inside his chest he saw the star so close he could reach out and touch it. He had reached the top of the mountain and the star was there with him.

As he reached out to touch the star he had climbed so high to reach Robert Carlyle awoke. He sat up in bed, his hair long enough now to touch his shoulders, he brushed it away from his face. He was very clear minded and knew that whatever the wish was that he might be wanting was going to have to be worked for. Then and there he was determined to set his goals and climb every step of the way to find his star. This would not be something one could simply wish for. He wished he would find what he was wishing for soon.

AULD LANG SYNE

Letting go. The embrace of new beginnings.

(I)

"How long have you known him?" Robert asked of Swansea. They were standing in the alleyway behind the house Bradly had provided for them. Neither of them was sure if it was Bradly's, stolen, some combination of the two... or rented out proper and legal. But it didn't matter, they had come to understand Bradly was capable of all those things and either way would not be questioned.

He took a long drag from his cigarette before he answered, his voice somehow thicker than the smoke coming out of his lungs, "Some time, I guess. Hard to say exact. But it wasn't until all of this that I put everything together." That drew a curious look from Robert, not in response to the information, but to the conclusion of his statement.

"Everything?"

"Oh god no, I was just sayin' some things were clearer. That's all." Swansea never was one to be on the defensive about his words. Even then he was telling Robert rather than explaining himself. He did not know, nor did he have the desire to know, everything there was about the ports and how they truly operated.

"I've always minded my business knowin' some things were not mean for me to know. I only look to find out what I need to in order

163

to stay in business and do what I enjoy doing. I don't give a shit about legal or not, but I follow the rules, y'know?"

Robert understood, but still wanted to hear, "The rules?"

"You know what I mean, boy. The unwritten rules. Some are following the law of the land, and some are following the law of the sea. Some are printed in a book and looked over by a badge… and others you learn along the way." Swansea brought the cigarette up to his mouth like a bronze statue in Paris, contemplating his past and seemingly going into memories he'd long stowed away deep beneath the floorboards of his mind.

"…and some you learn the hard way."

Robert leaned into the bricks he'd been next to and fell into contemplation about the man's words. "I imagine there are still some rules left to write."

"Aye." Swansea confirmed, "and some to redefine."

"Should we forgive them?"

"I'm not certain I know who any of them are besides Bradly." He took a long drag on his cigarette. "We know their names, but that doesn't tell us anything. All I know is there's steady work, I get to take in the salty air each day and am going to try and live out the rest of my days with the comfort of being under some people making some big decisions."

"They're not hiding much from us though. We're managing trade that's clearly illegal. Helping to mask things as passable when they're clearly not." Robert struggled to build a complete truth on the details he had.

Swansea muddied the waters further for them, "You're a smart kid. You know damn well there's a bigger picture and that we're not part of it." Robert left his thinking wall to listen more closely to the wisdom before him. "At least I won't ever be part of it, but you might. Hell, you are." He emphasized, "You see things. You can see how everything moves together and which way things will go."

Swansea was right. Robert first had thought this trading game was the entire process, but it was only the breaking waves on the surface. Bradly had given him enough clues already.

"You forgive them. You forgive everything they've ever done. Then you find a way, like you always do, to get the bigger picture and control it all." Robert was already flush with thoughts. "Just promise me one thing, son." He had Roberts full attention, "you'll leave me to captain whatever ships need to be moved. It's what's keepin' me alive."

It was about the most Swansea had ever said in one sitting and, exactly as one would have suspected, it was insightful and inspiring all at the same time. There was something more than illegal shipping. Robert knew the items themselves were high value, and the insurance premiums they capitalized on helped, too, but something else was at play. There was an excessive amount of money coming in and the work kept piling up. He didn't get the impression it was purely about money. More about power.

But he didn't see displays of power. Something was hidden. There was no government involvement that he knew of, and he didn't see any operations behind the scenes to put more pieces into the evaluation. He had to find a way to control the shipping industry that was greater than just having the most money in the game.

"Robert." The tone from Swansea had Bradly's full attention, "She came to visit me."

(II)

Cat Jones sat in her small room organizing stacks of money she'd acquired the best way she'd known how. The bills did not stack very well after spending so much time thrown in a bag which had been soaked in the ocean on occasion, but she'd had no trouble exchanging the money and spending it. She felt at least this way it didn't look like it was fresh off the print and bound in solid bricks like it was when she got it.

She estimated she had to throw out enough money to buy a large home due to its condition, but somehow still had enough to shake her head and smile at. For her, it was still more about how she had come about the money than the total amount… although she was quite content knowing with her lifestyle she was more likely to lose this cash than to ever spend it. And that she could lay low for a long time with it until she needed more.

The thrill of the chase and the taste of the sea, however, were what she actually needed. The cash was just a trophy of accomplishment. She put the money back into her bag and brought the shades down about the room. Closing the door, she fell into the calm quiet the home offered when her roommate was working.

Not long after, Olvidio came into the small Lisbon house excited about having another 4 day weekend, "Catrina!… Catrina? Are you here?!?" He looked around the living room although it took hardly even a first look to know that nobody was in the room. "I have good news for you!" he called again throwing his thick Spanish accent against her door, "…are you in there?"

She was. And she had heard him through her yoga, she just wasn't aware enough to respond. Yoga had quickly become a great love of hers and it had been Olvidio that had really brought it alive for her. She loved his company more than the stillness of yoga, but it was one of the few things these days she loved more than the peace she found in her yoga.

She thought a lot about Swansea and how he dropped his cigarette. She'd seen him without one, but never lose track of one in the middle of smoking it. It was so good to see him, but she worried something was weighing on his mind. And his was not a mind that allowed much to weigh upon it.

She broke her trance and finally addressed her excited host.

"I'm in here, just finishing an afternoon mantra."

"Oh! That's great to hear. Which one?" His inquiry seemed genuine enough, however he gave no time for Cat to respond, "Let's go for a ride. Grab your stuff because I want to go climbing. I think

I've figured out the problem we were working on." He knocked on her door. She quickly glanced at her bag to make certain it was closed.

"It's open"

"I think I've figured out the problem we were working on." He repeating as though the door had been a complete sound barrier. It took her a short moment to realize the "problem" he was addressing was a technical term he used for the pathway up the face of a rock.

"You work on the climbing problems, I'm just lucky enough to see what you're doing and can follow behind." She reminded him as she always did when he spoke about rock-climbing being a team sport.

"I couldn't do it without you, Catrina" he said with a smile turning on the lights without warning. "I've got 3 full days to spend getting up that problem. Do you have the weekend available?"

Cat had all the time in the world and loved that he never cared to notice, "I think I could spare the time away from work."

"I wanted to ride up there and camp. The weather looks like it'll be just about perfect."

"Ride?"

"Bicycles… obviously. What else would we ride? The train doesn't go up that way and we-"

She cut him off, "I still don't have a bicycle." She spoke knowing that he wouldn't remember this time as she hadn't the many times before she had mentioned it.

"We should fix that." He mentioned as he had the many times before when he didn't remember. "Oh well, we'll take the car."

'Like we always do' she thought, but only presented her excited friend with a smile and a nod. She hopped up from her yoga mat and started towards the bag she needed for the trip. She knew everything was already in the car that he needed but waiting for him to start looking for it was a small joy she found each time they traveled.

Taking her non-verbal commitment Olvidio's eyebrows raised and he allowed his excitement to really get going.

"I'll start packing the camping gear into the car, when you have what you need will you see what groceries we have to take with us?" He was almost too far away from her already to have his entire thought heard, but it was the same discussion they had each time they packed up. She would gather pasta and spices and different foods from the cabinet while Olvidio found everything he was looking for piece by piece in the car. Olvidio would decide his idea was so grand he needed to invite as many people as he knew. He would call everyone who worked at the coffee shop and had even the slightest clue about climbing. If you had ever mentioned to Olvidio that you had been hiking, or mistakenly used 'hike' as a verb referring to a trip to your kitchen from your bedroom in the middle of the night, he remembered somehow that you were an active member of an outdoor community. Fortunately, the little coffee shop that employed him also employed others who had a great love for the outdoors. Unfortunately, it meant that someone had to work, and they rarely made any trips together. Inevitably Olvidio would get a call from a co-worker who was headed out on a boat or up a mountain, but he would be working. And somehow the monotony of asking and excitement and planning, followed by disappointment were always the beginnings of their trips. They truly were a unique group.

As rarely as they made trips out together, they always shared the planning and the story telling about the trips. Just not always so much about the 'doing' parts. But they all spoke about all the trips they shared as though they all had been there. And their bonds within that little coffee shop were strong. Customers knew all the stories but didn't always know who exactly the stories belonged to. And their passion about what they had done only brought more nature-enthusiasts to join their little troupe, sign up for adventures and share in the splendor of telling a story to someone who listened as though they had been on the trip right next to them.

She'd had so many of her own adventures. Even with people she never thought she'd see again. And, unfortunately for them, some adventures that meant they'd never be seen by anyone again.

It was but one small adventure, but Curtis, Robert and Swansea had each made a significant impact on her life. Each in their own way.

Curtis wrapped his life around her most feminine side and exposed something in her she longed to have out in the open. Swansea was a father figure she'd never had, despite how remote and removed he always was.

Robert was another figure all together. He looked at her like he knew her. He had a familiarity with her that was uncanny. Unremarkable. And, despite the natural feeling, very untrue. She'd never met him. Ever. She had no idea if his infatuation with her would turn into fortune or misfortune.

Cat packed enough food for breakfast all three mornings and for sandwiches when they were climbing. She had packed and planned for meals before and had learned that Olvidio, exhausted from the climbing during the day, would opt out of cooking dinner and have a sudden epiphany that they should drive into town and get a big meal with lots of wine. He always felt he earned it.

"Is there anything left that I could help you with?" he asked as he hung up the phone and slipped it into his pocket with mild disappointment.

"Nope, we've got all the food we need for the trip and it looks like you've got all the camping and climbing gear packed up too." This was as close to an inventory as they would get. Cat had made it a point to go over everything on her own. If she started with a discussion about equipment or supplies, Olvidio would conclude that they needed much much more. His dreams were compact and precise, but the reality was he just needed to be outside.

"Would you believe we still had most of the equipment in the car already?"

"Most?" Cat asked in disbelief that it wasn't already all there.

"Yeah, I had a bag with bike tubes and pumps and new brakes in it… oh! and lights for a night ride! that I'm sure we would hate to have been without"

Cat made no effort to remind him about her bicycle situation.

"I called a few people to join us. They're always so excited about the chance to come but nobody can ever get their schedules cleared up." He started in what seemed like the strangest déjà vu of her life. "One day we'll all get out there and have at least a week together."

She was amazed at their ability to let everything go. They had no idea the evils in the world and the impact some people could have on them. That impact affected her so much she could never relax and 'just let go'.

Cat just nodded along as they climbed into the car; Olvidio in the driver's seat and her perched up in the passenger's side. She would ride along with the window down and her hand riding the waves of the wind like the hull of a boat along the ocean. He was still talking as he started the car.

"Next month the entire group wants to get out to The Geres." He began. "It'll be a tough hike, nearly 25 miles all the way around. I said not to take bikes as that would make it just too simple of an adventure. Also, I'm pretty certain there are some extreme areas that wouldn't be good for biking. Not everyone would be able to do it, anyway."

"That's amazing. A big accomplishment for anyone." She said as she turned her phone off and put it away. "You can count me in."

She was pretty sure it was a lie.

(III)

Curtis walked about his room more comfortably each day. He had a noticeable limp from both legs, although his legs gave him no direct problems. It was his feet that troubled him. At least one large gash on his left foot and two on his right were slow to heal. It made him look on land the way most men looked their first time out at sea.

But it was just pain now. The healing would continue as long as he did not reopen the wounds. His stitches were gone, and the scabs were solid, but the bottoms of his feet were extremely tender. He wondered often if there was permanent damage or if his sea legs would ever be given the chance to be at home again. Crutches gave moderate relief, but mostly to the foot he put no pressure on. He managed to find the right balance between moving quickly and slowly in order to relieve the pain in one foot or the other. He wished he could transfer all the pain into one side just to be able to choose one over the other, but if he was going to walk he had to put his feet on the ground. And so he did.

Bradly was working in his office when Curtis approached. It was the first time he'd left his room on his own when he wasn't doing physical therapy. "Good to see you on your feet, my friend."

"What's left of 'em, I guess. It still hurts, but not more than the pain of being stuck in a room..." Curtis look around as if he could see through the walls and into the neighborhood, "...in whatever city I happen to be in."

"You're in Lisbon... well, across the river from it." Bradly started to explain but got confused. "Perhaps this is still Lisbon, I don't know. But I do know I'm awfully glad to see you up."

Curtis made his way over to his friend and they clasped hands.

"I sure could use a pint."

"Those are some of the greatest words I've ever heard come out of your sea-loving mouth!" Bradly laughed the words out in a slew of excitement. "I'll get a car over and have us out..." he paused to consider if going out was the best idea, "you think it's ok to go out?"

"Fuck you ya prick!" Curtis retorted. "The only thing wrong with your idea is that you think I need a car. Let's go. Unless you've got us up somewhere that doesn't have a pub in walking distance. And if that's the case-"

Bradly gladly interrupted "Oh no, I know just the place. "Close enough to be familiar, and far enough away you can limp and bitch about the walk."

Curtis smiled, "Perfect, now let's go get enough to drink my bitching and limping are the last thing you're concerned about on the way back."

The two made their way gingerly down the steps to the road. Curtis could maneuver much better without slopes heading upwards or downwards. For most of the walk they discussed geography. Specifically, where they were in the world, how simple it would be to know what city they were in or should know which way was east. All, of course, in jest towards Bradly who knew none of it.

For these two it was like they were kids again. Laughing at each other's follies: Curtis and his injuries, Bradly with his happy-go-lucky sense of forgetfulness. Or perhaps it was just genuine unawareness. Either way, the two were best friends today as they were most of the days in between their hardships. However, those hardships came, directly from each other or somewhere else in life, they had no problems goofing around and learning to forgive.

They entered a pub like so many others. It was perfect. Just bright enough to see the seats and recognize the difference between a patron and a bartender. Dark enough to lose any guilt you'd walked in the door with.

Striking up a conversation with the Spanish blonde behind the bar, they tried to ask her opinion on what they should drink from around the area. She recognized their accents, and more so Bradly's dark red hair, and quickly let them know theirs was the best Guinness in all of Spain.

The two men from Dublin quickly recognized a challenge, laced with a little flirting, and took her up on it. They took their pints, Curtis with his crutches and Bradly sipping off the tops of both, towards a table near a dark window back in the pub.

The laughter and forgetfulness gave them a sense of intoxication before they came in and had carried the light-heartedness up until they both had a few swallows of this Irish nectar. Somehow the mood fell into a lull and they stared off past each other... lost in the moment. Bradly spoke first to break the silence.

"I hated seeing you in so much pain."

Curtis looked up and down again acknowledging the statement. It was the equivalent of a full embrace between the two of them. And though they were not men who showed it, their compassion and reverence for each other was about to increase.

"Some of this was my fault. I knew you were bringing that Pearson to Gibraltar."

Curtis stayed stoic. Bradly knew this stirred so many emotions and additional questions he could not answer. But he continued forward with caution to what he was saying. And although there were some things he should never tell Curtis, and perhaps some things he would say anyway, in this moment he wanted nothing more than to have his friend back. He said to his old friend the only thing he could think to say.

"I'm so sorry, mate. I'm so sorry that all of this happened."

Curtis looked him square in the eye and stopped him from continuing his apology. They both looked down softly and contemplated the weight of the moment sitting between them at that table. Curtis finally, after a few pulls on his pint, looked over at the window.

"I don't suppose I'll ever know all the reasons why what happened happened. But if you're a true friend, and I believe you are, then I want nothing more than to put it behind us and move forward."

Bradly looked up at Curtis, and Curtis back at him. The stone-cold honestly between them gave them both reassurance towards the future. Curtis nodded once to assure his friend that all would be okay.

Bradly began the old traditional cheers in a manner neither of them had ever considered.

"Should old acquaintance be forgot, and never brought to mind?
Should old acquaintance be forgot, and old lang syne?"

Curtis fell in line knowing exactly the timely essence of the poem.

"For auld lang syne, my friend, for auld lang syne,
We'll take a pint of Guinness yet, for auld lang syne.
And surely, you'll buy your pint, and surely you'll buy mine!
And we'll take a pint o' Guinness yet, for auld lang syne."

They clashed their pints together and Bradly continued,
"We two have paddled in the stream, from morning sun till dine;
But seas between us broad have roared since auld lang syne.
There's a hand my trusty friend! And give me a hand o› thine!

Curtis had his hand firmly clasped against his friends before the verse
was finished. Together they finished the tradition and the first pint
of a memorable night.

"And we'll take a right good-will draught, for auld lang syne."

FORESHADOWING

New decisions that mean everything.

(I)

The cards leaped one over the other in front of him as he followed the red ace. The man on the street stopped after a few quick gestures back and forth. "Sir, do you know where the red card is?"

Robert pointed quickly to the middle card. A sly smile and a quick flip from the man behind the table revealed Robert's guess was correct. "You have a quick eye my friend!" he complimented his mark not knowing that Robert was on to his game.

"Let's try again, this time a little faster." He winked and held the cards upright for all to see, "there's the red ace and there are the two black kings." He dropped one black king to the table face down, and with one hand he showed the ace again to Robert, "see if you can follow it." Turning the cards over, he flung a card down followed by the final card from his hand. He immediately went into his routine of one card over the other.

"Try to keep up… she needs you."

Robert couldn't help but look up at the dealer, "What did you say?"

"Keep up, don't lose the red card!" He slowed down not wanting the man before him to stop following the cards as, with no money on the table, he needed him to be able to win a few times in a row before the magic began.

"Ok, where's the red ace?"

Robert, certain he'd just imagined things, pointed to a card the dealer was hovering way too much towards.

Relieved, the dealer flipped over the red ace, "Excellent! You're a wiz here. Would you like to make it more interesting with a little wager?" He hoped his bait was out enough to lure in a big catch.

"Of course." Robert knew the game and enjoyed the challenge. He would watch how the hustler held the 2 cards to see if he dropped the lower one or released the top card. If he caught that, then following the right card was not difficult at all. It had everything to do with catching which card was released from his hand: the one he showed or the one he was hiding. Both cards were there, the sleight of hand came at the beginning of the trick.

Robert grabbed his wallet, pulled a few bills out, but, most importantly, displayed to the hustler that there was more cash remaining. He knew he would let him win the first hand or two, it was just a matter of timing for adding the cash and hustling the hustler.

Again, all the cards were displayed. It was clear there were two black kings and a red ace. The dealer took two in one hand and the third in the other. Displaying the cards again, he dropped one of the kings and reminded everyone watching to follow the red ace. The cards hit the table and the shuffle began. Robert noted which card fell first and tracked it easily.

"Don't lose her, Robert. She's the reason you came this far."

Robert tried hard to follow the obvious card but was instantly troubled by what he thought he heard. He tucked his hair behind his ears, it was longer than he'd ever had it before and it was getting out of control.

"Sir." The man spoke again without a hint of knowing his real name, "are you following the red one?... let's see." The shuffle stopped, and the man smiled wide hoping its location was obvious and Robert was willing to make a bet.

Robert, still stunned at what he was hearing, refocused when another viewer beside him clearly bet on the wrong card. He glanced over at the false player he suspected was only there to make him feel more comfortable about his bet.

"The red card is here." Robert placed some bills over another card where he had followed the red ace.

The dealer flipped the card without a bet, revealing a black king, "Someone's got a good eye!" Flipping the cards, the red ace was under Robert's money and an equal amount was awarded. Robert collected it and started to put the money in his wallet.

"Wait wait wait!!" cried the street magician. "I know you're good, but you gotta give me a shot to make my own money back." Robert, feeling he had the upper hand, reached back into his wallet showing his willingness to reconsider.

Glad about seeing the window was still open, he readied the cards. "You can't give up on her. You know the truth and it's up to you to save her."

This time Robert knew what he heard. "What do you know?"

"I know you're willing to take a chance, but is it for the right woman? Do you think you can really save her?" He showed the cards again. Threw one down like before and showed the remaining two: one red, one black. He began the game throwing the cards quickly one over the other. The shuffle moving faster than any of the previous times.

"You obviously think she's still there, but perhaps you have her confused with someone else."

Robert's mind was racing as he followed the cards. He couldn't believe what he was hearing. Did this stranger know who Samantha was? Did he know Cat? And how did he know about both of them...?

His hands stopped moving, leaving three cards face down on the table.

"Are you willing to risk everything?"

Robert pulled the remaining money from his wallet and put everything on the card farthest to the right. He didn't even take the time to count how much he had bet. He didn't care. At this point he felt his honor was being challenged. Like this stranger could see the past and the future and was pulling Robert further and further into some unwanted controversy. He was certain everything he was doing was for Samantha. He didn't feel that this was selfish at all, and he wanted to help Cat just like anyone else. Not just because they looked alike.

The dealer flipped the first card, farthest away from Robert's attempt, revealing a red queen of hearts.

"You can't save her, Robert. You just can't." He flipped the middle card revealing another red card, the queen of diamonds. "The cards look the same at first glance, but obviously they're different.

He took the money off the final card and flipped it over revealing a king.

Robert awoke suddenly and looked for the time. "Fuck! I'm late!" he cried as he jumped from his bed and quickly put on the pants he'd taken off the night before and left on the floor. He then sat on the bed, hands on head, and closed his eyes. He only allowed himself the moment, however, to contemplate the curiosities that took over his dreams lately. But he had to get to the docks quickly. Swansea may have already left without him. Knowing how the old sailor could get so focused on the task at hand, the clock was not always considered.

(II)

Swansea was not even on the ship when Robert approached him on the dock.

"It's the first time I've ever known you to be late." He said to Robert without even looking up from his clipboard.

"You would have to have looked at a clock to know that, and that's not like you at all." Robert replied getting the sense that something happened negating his need for timeliness at all. "I get the feeling I don't need to run an inspection on this load? Should I even walk the ship for the principle of it all?"

Swansea held up his clipboard, showing not much paperwork clipped to it at all, "There really isn't anything to inspect."

Robert looked at how low the shipping vessel was in the water and back at the ship's captain standing in front of him, "That ship is sitting pretty low in the water not to have anything aboard it needing inspection." He knew there was a bigger game these days, and that more than half of his inspections weren't anything more than show. His role was to verify weight against expected weight, calculate shipping times, and the overall expenses of the dock's shipping and receiving. However, it was rare that his role and what he actually did landed on the same page.

Sarcasm, however, was often lost on Swansea. "You know damn well this ship is full of stock and ready to go." He corrected. "My job is to captain these ships regardless of what is on them. That doesn't change if I'm shipping toys, cars or whatever the hell is in these crates. Your job..." he paused, realizing he was working himself up over nothing, "your job is to say that whatever's on the ship is the same as what's on the paper. And whoever is on the ships is on the ships. Even when it's not."

"It's a little more complicated than that," Robert defended weakly, "but especially more complicated when there isn't any paperwork to help me pretend to do a job with." Swansea gave him what little documents he had regarding this load.

"Well, yeah. Bradly already has the other sheets. I'm pretty sure the sellers took the overboard insurance guaranteeing almost immediate delivery to the bottom of the sea and replacement crates filled with whatever Bradly and his group are moving around the world." Swansea stopped his ramble and let Robert know what he needed to know. "They're all up on the ship, by the way, talking about something important. It's the whole reason I'm staying on land until I'm given the green light to head out."

"Are they all up there?" He asked Swansea.

"I don't know who *all* of them are, but the one woman who seems to run the show. Some guy who's always around and one of their goons."

"Just one of them? Not feeling very threatened today, are they?"

"If only needing one bodyguard means you're taking a break from being insecure, I guess that's one way to look at it. And it's not like you're a threat to them." Swansea was never good at passing humor.

Robert pulled his hair back tight and with clean confidence twisted it behind his head. It was dark and full, and now that it was up and out of his face, he took control away from the wind and commanded the moment like an executive, "I'm no threat to their health, that's for sure. But I've got some ideas about their business practices."

"Good luck with that."

Robert nodded and made his way up onto the ship. He was confident Swansea meant what he said about the luck.

(III)

Although the scars on the bottoms and sides of Curtis' feet would always give him a physical reminder of his injuries, walking had again become something common in his life. The scars on the mind of Bradly for having ultimately caused Curtis' injuries, however, would pain him nearly every step he took for the rest of his life. The guilt he held drove his compassion and protection of Curtis.

Only a week had past, and Curtis found himself able to do mundane jobs for Bradly. Only now it was out in the open and no more theft… officially. Bradly would not let him out of his sight, and Curtis found himself doing more actual work than he had ever done. The pay was nice, too. Bradly even gave a subtle bonus to Curtis without warning. Curtis thought it was out of guilt, and he wasn't wrong, just he wasn't completely correct. He was kept in the dark about the truth going on, especially what Robert was up to. Bradly was restricted from including him too much but made sure that many of the ships needing to make it to their destination, more so than others, would be loaded by the trustworthy friend he'd had for so long. The extra money he received from these recent transactions turned into the extra cash Curtis would receive. So, in a way, Curtis was earning those bonuses without ever knowing what the product was.

Curtis knew. Enough. He didn't need to learn any more.

He had learned quickly the level of authority that Bradly had over these shipments. He wasn't just a longshoreman. Or a longshoreman's supervisor. The money was good, and he didn't feel like he was doing the wrong thing. He was okay just being part of it all. He missed the rush of boat theft, but the fact everything he was doing wasn't exactly legal, gave him just enough to secure his fix and go about life in his normal.

Bradly and Curtis had started to find a rhythm. Bradly was on the docks more often to learn from Curtis and tended to give Curtis more information than he needed to have. Right or wrong, today was especially part of that inclusion.

Curtis was outmatched by the previous knowledge in the room, "Isn't that run by the Spanish?" Bradly was there with a woman and two other men.

"Not the northern side." Bradly informed him, "We own that."

"We?" Curtis looked around the room.

"Well, the British do."

"So… Spain controls nothing?"

"They control the southern side."

"But that's not Spanish land." Curtis remarked.

"Ownership and control are different things. In fact, *we* don't actually *own* any of that, but we are in control of everything being built there." Said the balding man in a suit who was the only other participant in the conversation so far.

Curtis suddenly felt validated in his observations. He had thought the judgment coming from the others was too much. Perhaps

181

it was just their stoicism listening to a loudmouth tell his friend too many secrets. "…isn't that going to take decades? You're talking about building all the way across the Strait of Gibraltar. That's gotta be pretty fucking far."

Bradly haphazardly took control of the conversation back, "It's only about 9 miles. And the estimate is a century."

"Then why bother?" Curtis didn't understand.

Bradly continued despite the unapproving looks of the others in the room, "Because the majority of the work is already done." He had Curtis stunned with the idea. "They began in the 1920's when Germany thought they could build a dam, control the waters, and ultimately repopulate land for Europeans when the Mediterranean Sea evaporated."

Curtis was confused, "Is this public information?"

"Some of it." He confirmed, "But only the plans. The fact is that the infrastructure was actually built across the Camarinal Sill some time ago. That's a well-kept secret. Even better, my father created the additional design about 30 years ago to complete the nine miles across the Strait of Gibraltar."

Of the three others in the room, Sandra, whose emotions were a better kept secret than the one being told now in front of her, shifted uneasily from one foot to the next. Bradly was too caught up in the moment and Curtis rarely applied his intelligence to interpreting what other's thought of him.

"I always knew your dad deserved his job, I just never figured out what he had done to get it." Curtis concluded openly and looked over those he didn't know, "Is he part of this whole thing?"

"No." She said coldly.

Bradly defended his father, "No, he could never get beyond the construction of the central dam."

"Central dam? I thought it was going to go all the way across."

"It will." Bradly corrected himself, "I mean, it does. But only between the major currents like a belt. It's in the middle from left to right, not in the middle between the two coasts. It's not at the surface and it only touches the bottom where it is fixed against the seabed." He paused to catch his breath, "We're almost ready to expand it and either stop the Atlantic from going in, or the Mediterranean from going out. We need to figure out what will happen, and who will be benefit the most from the changes."

Curtis hadn't a clue. He knew what to do when tides shifted, or waves rose above what was expected, but he couldn't predict the unknown.

Bradly looked out and saw Robert approaching. "That's him now." The others paused and looked out at the man approaching. They knew of him only through Bradly, but the adjustments he'd already made recently showed he held a sense of understanding about the entire project already. "If anyone can decipher what we know and predict what will happen... it's him."

Curtis took advantage of the pause in conversation. "Excuse me for a moment, I need to find a restroom." A familiar nod was exchanged between him and Robert and they passed by each other.

Robert entered the room seeing some familiar faces, but no one he'd had the opportunity to get to know very well. He did, however, know that this particular group was well informed and might be the best way to learn more about the bigger business. He was right, and they were thinking the same thing about the business and their opportunities with him.

He broke the ice, "According to the current level of the ship in the water, I'm missing some paperwork."

Bradly interjected trying to prove his own point to his superiors against Robert's sarcasm, "He's a quick one. But more importantly," he looked back confidently to say his next point, "he can help review where the Atlantic currents might be heading and where they are not."

Robert did not see the immediate puzzle they were asking him to solve, "Satellite imagery has already mapped the Atlantic currents. Even against climate change, it's pretty easy to see what warmer waters will bring to the future of shipping."

The suited man spoke up again, "Glad you've already taken into consideration what the natural future holds." Bradly shrunk, realizing he was no longer going to lead the conversation moving forward and resigned to a wall. "We want you to consider what will happen when we start to control certain areas of major water flow."

Now he was intrigued.

Robert, unlike Curtis, did not dive headfirst into theories or suggestions, "I'm going to need some more details. There're too many factors in the oceans. Some big, some small. But all contributors." Even without a full understanding, he was taking control, "We definitely see a significant change in fuel expenses depending on which way we ship. And we're about to start charging based on exactly that. Time is money, you know."

"Exactly the entire point. Time." Sandra looked excited, "He's much smarter than the other one, Bradly." She apparently only spoke up to emphasize a known point and her position near the top.

Bradly remembered his place, "Curtis is a good man, and a loyal friend."

"He's a thief!" She fired back, "and you'd be wise to question the loyalty of anyone that close to you."

Robert took control, "How about we control the things we can control right here and right now?" The control room of the ship fell silent except for the hum of the engine and some electrical equipment. "I'm not saying that information should be freely handed out, but I'm confident you have people to take care of that when it becomes a problem. Right now, I believe, my strengths are something you'd like to bring into the mix. So, I'd need some more information and I hope you're willing to share."

"Fair enough, Robert." Her's was the voice of reason, control and authority. "You're right. If Bradly here has shared too much, the problem will be solved. We are too far along in the process to be interrupted, but we still want to manage every detail to maximize our potential." She looked at the silent strength standing beside her.

The thick man nodded with understanding, and Bradly swallowed as considering what he might have already done to his friend.

She continued, "Surely you've heard of me as I've heard of you. My name is Sandra. This is one of my business partners Juan Sebastián, he manages most of the analytics for the *bigger* project we have underway." Robert noticed pretty clearly that she did not introduce the muscle. "You could say I control the partnerships and overall direction we are headed. We've learned a lot about you from what we've seen with your professionalism and insight. We also know from Bradly you've concluded quite a bit about our operations on the docks here and at other ports."

Robert looked towards Bradly realizing his position of power was far less than he previously thought. Bradly stood taller for just a moment feeling he'd done something right.

"However, after listening to Bradly talk with our friend Curtis, who's to say what Bradly learned from you and what you learned from him." Bradly's confidence faded. "Now" she continued back with Robert, "We don't actually know much about you or where you came from and have had difficulty with your history. Anything you'd like to clarify?"

Robert wasn't interested. He had learned enough to know he was on the right track but was not familiar enough with the players in the game to know who to trust. "To be completely honest, Sandra, I'd prefer we all focus on what we can gain from this relationship and, if things go well, we can get to know each other sometime in the future. I image that time is of the essence, yes?"

She liked his style. Ready to proceed she opened up the conversation, "Juan Sebastián. If you don't mind."

He popped into action producing blue prints and maps which he laid out in front of Robert. "Where we are focused is on the large currents flowing to and from the Atlantic Ocean and the Mediterranean Sea. As you see here, it's not going to be a problem to actually build a structure across the Gibraltar Strait and control the flow of water in and out."

"Like a hydroelectric dam? You'd be able to power much of the continent."

"Yes" he continued, "but that's not a major issue just a positive side effect. What we are looking to do is control much of the ocean's current and the shipping between India, Europe and the Americas."

Robert was amazed at the potential, "You have the potential to determine how fast, or how slowly, shipping vessels moved through the Atlantic. Doubling or tripling the amount of time it took for large cargo ships to arrive at one port from another."

Sandra chimed in for the much bigger picture, "Yes, Robert. And more importantly, this type of change will affect some weather patterns. We need to know what climates we'd control and who would need to pay us in order to protect their lands from sudden changes on their coastlines."

(IV)

"That's incredible!" Cat Jones exclaimed nearly losing the phone she had wedged between her cheek and her shoulder. Her hands were busy loading bullets into a magazine. She paused her chore, put the magazine next to the gun on the bed next to her, and reached up to shift the phone over to her other ear. "And I thought all the illegal shipping was somehow linked to human trafficking."

She filled the magazine and clicked it into the pistol while listening to the other side of the conversation, "Yeah. Obviously." She waited again, seemingly eager to state a point that had been missed. "At the end of the day I'm going to get paid. Yes, you, too. And a whole lot more than you're getting now. We just need to find some proof. Some names. Some details. And if they're all there now, we might be able to find something."

Cat pulled a second gun from a bag placing it on the bed like she was doing inventory. She lined up a smaller backpack and two holsters. "Of course I trust you." She listened. "No, I just think I need to be there, too. You're expected to… you know, work. But you can let me know where they are or what areas it's safe to be in. I can make the entire voyage, it's fine."

Frustration was showing as it became less of an operation and more of a personal conversation. Then she stood up, "Robert is there? With them? Like, talking to them and getting to know them? Why aren't you in the room?" She was practically yelling at this point. Clearly, she knew that the information she was getting was nothing compared to what could be learned during this phone call.

Before she could fully consider the choices made on the timing of the call, Olvidio came in suddenly, "Are you ok?"

His face seemed to stop in time looking down at the guns laid out on Cat's bed. There were extra clips and more ammunition along with the climbing gear they had just used the past weekend. "I heard yelling, I'm sorry." He couldn't stop staring at the situation. Cat put the phone down, clearly the point had been made and now she had something else to deal with.

She remained silent, watching and waiting to learn her roommate's perspective and to gauge the amount of trust she could put into him. She mentally reviewed how much knowledge about her he had and what someone might be able to learn if he was questioned.

"Catrina, what is all this?" She refused to answer such an obvious question. If he were a target, he'd be laid out by now. But he wasn't. Not in the slightest. He was the most amazing escape from reality she'd ever known and had hoped this relationship might have turned into an actual friendship. That thought was fading now. She was straining for a way to let him live knowing her name and, now, some idea of what her work might have been. She wasn't going to be able to convince him she was just a gun-enthusiast. Not here. Not now. Not like this.

"Olvidio." She used his name to quell the situation. She often used that kind of information to distract her mark, but not this time. "I won't pretend this is normal or expected, but I need you to stay calm and tell me what's going through your mind?" She needed to know his instinct about all of this and if he could be trusted. Was he drawing conclusions or just shocked? Would he share this as public knowledge, or would he be so frightened he'd block it out and try his damnedest to continue as he always had?

He was simple, but his honesty and integrity might win over her hope for his loyalty and naivety. Without looking down, Cat silenced an incoming phone call, put the phone in her pocket and both hands slowly up hoping to calm her friend.

"Olvidio, I'm in no danger. This is all for my protection for something I need to do." She was counting on his compassion being directed more towards her safety than his own. "You know me. You know me so well. I'm not going to hurt anyone. Do you understand?"

"That's not what it looks like." Not wanting to make him concentrate any harder than he already was, she waited for him to put his own thoughts together. His eyes moved from one piece of equipment to another. He focused just as much on the two guns as he did the backpack and the climbing gear. If he was considering things familiar to him as well as the weapons, he must be trying to figure out the bigger picture. That was good. Catrina wasn't about to let him know more than he already did, but if he was able to consider more than what was immediately in front of him, he might live to not tell about this.

He finally started to articulate his thoughts, "It just looks like you have a lot more going on that I ever imagined. I never thought you were simple, Catrina, but I thought you were in sales or something. You know?" She felt the room lighten up a little. She loosened her guard, let her hands down towards her sides and took a step towards him.

"It's like sale: I acquire things and make money of those items. I just don't buy them first." She was hoping some levity was called for. Olvidio wasn't ready to laugh, and possible never ready to laugh about this moment, but he was breathing much more normally now.

"I thought for a second you were an assassin. Out there killing people. I've seen what you can do leaping from one position to another when we climb, so perhaps you're a ninja? I don't know."

She smiled at his innocence, but not so much that she continued trying to make the situation something it was not. He was smarter than that and she wasn't going to insult him. But she did want to give him enough to keep his wits, and his life, about him.

"I'm no assassin. Sometimes I get things I know are worth money, and sometimes I'm paid to go get things that are worth something to others. Either way, it's a job well done when nobody even realizes the job is over."

"So, you're a thief. That's not good either."

"I'm not saying it's good. I understand what it is. But I promise you I don't put myself in situations I shouldn't be in." Her mind instantly remembering several cases that did just the opposite. "What I need to know is that this stays here." He was silent now considering that he knew anything that might put him in danger.

"I won't ask any questions."

"Good. That's a great start. I'm not going to tell you anything you shouldn't know and there's nobody who's going to be looking for me. At least not here."

He began, "but if the police come by and-"

She felt like she had control now and was ready to guide him where he needed to be, for her safety and for his. "Right or wrong, Olvidio, the people who would be looking for me are not in any way part of the police. In fact, the police would probably thank me for the jobs that I take."

"Oh, you're like Robin Hood, then?"

"Not exactly" she laughed a little but was mostly relieved he was headed in that direction. "Look, I need to get off to somewhere while some people… are… not where they're supposed to be." She gathered herself and made some decisions.

"I won't be coming back here for a while. And I won't have a way for you to contact me. I'm going to leave some things that I'll come back for." She felt this was insurance on his loyalty if he thought she could return at any moment. She had one more way to buy his loyalty just in case, "I'm going to give you some money, too."

"I'm not going to say anything, Catrina. I just want to know you're ok."

"I'll be fine. Trust me." She reached into a bag and brought out a stack of money. She didn't know how much it was, and even though she had more, she counted off a specific amount just to give the idea of calculation. "Here, take it. Not for your silence, I think you'll do that just for me." She was confident now. "Take it for your generosity. Everything you've already done for me up until this point. I feel I owe it to you."

He took the money, and as he did she took his hands in both of her. He took a deep breath and sighed. Once she felt the moment solidified, she smiled big, "Now, I've got to gather some things and be on my way."

"Do you need a ride?" It was as if he was totally on her side now without a fear in the world.

"Oh my god that would save me so much time. Would you mind?"

LOVES

(I)

Curtis felt worthless just standing there. Not too long ago he felt like he was making moves and showing how important he could be. Now he just listened to Robert and Juan Sebastián go back and forth. For him it was like listening to two elementary children discuss some imaginary world nobody else knew about. He only followed half of what they were saying, and that's just because they were speaking in his own language and mentioned places on a map he'd been to recently.

In reality, Curtis was the elementary kid trying hard to keep up with a bigger conversation. In fact, most of the people in the room were. With Juan Sebastián's data and Robert Carlyle's perceptions, it was hard to keep up. These were the discussions that needed to be held in order to take the project to the next level. Robert was proving himself and Curtis was watching it in real time.

"Show me again how the dam works. I get that it will only stop either the water rushing in from the Atlantic, or the heavier water flowing westward from the Mediterranean, but why not both?"

Juan Sebastián pulled a different set of blueprints to reference. "To be short, we just don't trust the stability of the dam to handle pressure from the top and pressure from the bottom at the same time. We only choose to deploy the walls towards the seabed *or* the surface.

It's not like a regular dam where the pressure only helps to reinforce the sturdiness of it all."

"But that's why it's built *into* the Camarinal Sill." Robert said thinking he proved his point.

"That steadies the engineering in one direction. Not two."

Robert's command of tone clarified as much as his words did, "And because the main points are centered on the edges, not the middle…"

"Like a jump rope." Curtis shot in unexpectedly. All eyes immediately went to him. "It's fixed on the sides but can move freely in the middle." He felt sheepish, but still confident. "Only this jump rope is nine miles long and made of steel and concrete. And can deploy plates above or below it… nevermind." He tried to back out.

"No, that's a good point, Curtis." Robert simultaneously tried to protect his honor and justify his position. "With strong currents on top and bottom, and with it fixed centrally left to right, the whole thing might just start spinning in place and not be true to its engineering."

"Is that true, Juan Sebastián?" Sandra asked. Curtis hoped his interjection helped. "Is that why they couldn't just dam the area where two large bodies of water met."

"Yes, but we know all of that already." Juan Sebastián replied to her but strained to the group. "What we don't know is how either stoppage of the water flows would affect the Atlantic Currents. We have a real good idea of what will happen in the Mediterranean if you remove, or add, large amounts of water. But the rise or fall of the Atlantic would be minor. It's the flow of water we're concerned about."

"I got it, I got it." Robert's eyes lit up like he'd downloaded decades of research in the past hour or so. "Let's look again at the surface currents in the Atlantic."

Juan Sebastián pulled out a map with tiny arrows all over the details on the ocean.

"No, not just the North Atlantic, both North and South." Robert corrected.

"But the Mediterranean is in the North, Robert." He justified.

"The current flow on both hemispheres is at play here. And the amount of influence coming from what you're trying to do, will impact both the parts of that giant ocean."

Robert was right. They were only focused on the ports and directions of the current flow mainly between North America and Europe. To get a better feel of what would happen, you had to consider all the doors, or valleys, the water might flow towards.

Robert, now with the full map, began to speculate.

"The currents make two opposite swirls starting from the equator. The Northern Atlantic waters move clockwise, and the Southern Atlantic waters move counterclockwise. It's like the water is coffee, and the equator is the spoon. When you move a spoon backwards across the cup, swirls happen on both sides, but in opposite directions." Curtis was very much intrigued now.

Juan Sebastián almost looked disappointed, "That would mean the spinning of the earth has far more influence than the current. We won't make a change at all."

Robert nodded, consenting some of what he heard to be true, "In the grand scheme of things, no, you're not going to compete with earth's rotation. But we will influence it. Right now, the balance between the current flows over the Strait of Gibraltar are neutral. But if you allow the Atlantic Ocean to flow a little more easterly…"

Juan Sebastián followed along, "The Northern Atlantic will swirl in the same direction, but slower."

"Yes, exactly. And if we open up the Mediterranean to flow out into the same path the Atlantic is already moving in…"

"The entire process would speed up. It's so simple."

Sandra was impressed. "So, we can control how fast things are going, but not change the direction."

Robert looked confident. Clearly, he didn't want to oversee ships any longer. He wanted the entire thing. He was taking it. He was ready to control the oceans and everything in them. "If we really want to predict what will happen, we need a way to track heavy objects, like a boat, moving only along the top current. All these maps and charts show satellite images and trajectories, but we really need to track something moving along without anything influencing its movement but the wind and the surface waves."

"We've already done that." Bradly finally added to the conversation.

All eyes moved to him, whether they followed his exact meaning or not.

"We had a Pearson 424 go without any mechanical influence from Dublin, all the way down the coast, and into mouth of the Mediterranean Sea. He crossed the Strait of Gibraltar and we took note of how long it took. Piece of cake."

Curtis was stunned. He thought it had everything to do with the boat, not him.

"Curtis, did you ever start that motor?"

"No ma'am. Absolutely not." He said assuredly. "But I didn't know why I was doing it."

She looked away and stopped addressing him directly. "If he had known, who knows who he would have told. Or who knows who might have figured him out. And now he knows a lot more than just why he was floating down a current." Bradly looked away from his childhood friend and over at this woman he suddenly feared more than anything.

"It wasn't like he was pretending it was his own ship when we were on board with him." Robert added to the mix, further proving Curtis was no secret keeper. "We were aware of this thief right from the start. Even if he kept him mouth shut he could keep no secrets."

Curtis was speechless. He'd wished he had been like that for much longer than just the past few moments. Bradly took his shot, "We scared the shit out of him in Lisbon. He knows we're serious and he's got the scars to remind him. Isn't that enough for you all?"

Sandra reminded Bradly that his objective was not just to scare Curtis that day.

"Until this is controlled, we can't let anyone know who isn't part of what we're doing." Robert spoke as if it were his idea from the beginning. "Governments would shut us down and dismantle what we have. We need more than just the construction happening beneath the surface of the water. We need to build alliances based on proof we can do what we say we can do. We need to control, not just the ports, but the actions between the ports and we must show that we are in control or we will lose everything."

Sandra had found the missing piece and, until that moment listening to Robert, never felt more like the entire gamble would pay off. A slow smile found its place with her as he put out an ultimatum.

"...and I'll be damned if I let anyone learn how we are controlling the waters."

(II)

Swansea was working a deck broom up and down the rows between the cargo. It was the best he could do considering the meeting upstairs was keeping him from starting his delivery.

He hated it.

Not what was being discussed or what they were aiming to do, he just hated that it kept him from doing his job. Everything was completed, and this deck was as good as it was going to get. But he knew his place and knew he had a good thing going for himself. He asked no questions and was the best alibi anyone could need. He said very little to authorities and gave away nothing. He was willing to give up his cargo if needed. In fact, at the right price or persuasion, he'd even be convinced to give up his crew. It had happened before and, somehow, he was the one still standing here.

What did he have to lose?

He had time and he had his tobacco. If the ship were moving he'd probably be doing the exact same thing only somewhere out in the middle of the Atlantic.

He leaned the broom against the front of a large red cargo box and tucked back in between two others to strike a match. The flame was as tall as the match to begin but died down to about the size of the end of his cigarette. He commanded the flame about as well as he could command a ship. Wind and weather might move the mighty element, but he knew how to keep the ship upright and the fire going. It was like he'd done it before. Only it never became mindless. His focus was razor sharp when it came to the things that were most important to him.

Watching his surroundings, however, was never something he was as good at as he should have been. He had dropped the match and took his first drag off his smoke when an arm wrapped quickly around his neck and he felt a blade poke his skin right underneath his chin. As his cigarette fell his eyes followed it. His vision tracked the falling ember with more concern for his nicotine fix than the knife held to his throat. He got over his worry for his cigarette pretty quickly.

"How many are up there?"

He was still stunned by the situation and could not speak. He felt the restraint loosen just a little.

"I know they're in the room, but how many of them are there? And how many bodyguards?"

Swansea recognized the voice.

"Cat?"

"Shut the fuck up and answer me, old man. I don't want to hurt you. I know you have nothing to do with this."

"Cat, if you'd just let me go I'd tell you whatever you need to know"

She tightened her grip but sheathed the knife. They both knew she wouldn't use it on him. "And, you'll tell me what I need to know while I have you in this 'thinking hold'. I need you to focus and give me the details I asked for."

It was hard for him to consider anything other than what she wanted to know as his air flow was being threatened. He didn't even have the time to consider that was exactly why she was doing it.

"There are five of them. Robert, Bradly and three others. Robert just joined them about an hour ago."

"Bradly? Bradly O'Sheel?"

She let him go. He had barely reached for his neck to comfort the strain as he also reached down to grab the cigarette at his feet.

"You lied to me, Swansea."

"I didn't fucking lie to you, Cat. Besides, you fucking had me in a choke hold. What the fuck are you thinking?"

"You'll thank me for that choke hold when they ask questions later." She justified her actions, "Curtis is up there. There are six of them."

"What?" He was shocked. He was still having a hard time realizing what she said and how she counted so quickly.

"Curtis. He's up there, too. You told me only five people were there. You trying to get me killed?"

"Cat, I'm only trying to breathe. I forgot about Curtis. God damn it." He was getting back to his usually self. The very person she was trying to avoid at the start of this. "You're going about this the wrong god damned way. How did you know Curtis was there?"

She wasn't here to dive deep into any conversation.

"How many bodyguards?" She barely paused. "Damn it, old man, how many? I'm serious here. Shit is going down that needs to be stopped."

"Just one."

He looked down the ship the other way considering if anyone else was on the ship he should tell her about.

"I can't think of anyone else on board."

But she was already gone, and on her way up to see some previous acquaintances.

(II)

Curtis looked down at his phone anxiously.

"You expecting a call, friend?" Bradly asked.

"No. Just checking the time."

The two of them were taking advantage of Robert and Sandra walking out of the main cabin into the captain's quarters nearby. They looked through the blueprints on the table but were hesitant to look at anything that hadn't been left visible already.

Juan Sebastián cautioned them with a reminder of what having too much information would lead to.

"Knowing details isn't really the problem, Juan. It's telling other people. And nobody here is going to be sharing this information with anyone."

Curtis was silent.

"They'll make sure of it. And you know that better than anyone, Bradly."

Curtis was getting very uncomfortable. There was no level of curiosity that would allow him to forget what he'd already seen.

And what he'd already shared.

He wanted to ask forgiveness, but fortunately his logic was stronger than his conscience. At least right now it was. Admitting it would lead to certain death. How was he going to undo what he had done? He struggled with worry and figured the best place to clear his mind was out at sea.

"Seriously, you waiting for a call or what?"

Curtis had his phone out again without thinking.

"Uh…no. Really no. Hey, when can I get another assignment? Something long. What about solo-sailing the rest of the Atlantic Current?"

"Man, I don't know." Bradly told him truthfully. "I didn't know the purpose of the last one, just the task itself. And I sure as hell didn't know what the ending of that trip was going to be like." Guilt flooded over him. "At least not until we were already in Lisbon."

Curtis had nothing to say. He didn't even accidentally look at his phone.

"Look, it's not like you can't do all that on your own. It doesn't have to be official."

"But now it feels helpful. Now that I know why I was doing it, I'm a contributor. If I do it on my own, I'll just be a thief." His point was made. "…again."

"If you made that entire trip without motorization, they would absolutely be able to use that data. Whether they commissioned the trip or not. Right Juan?"

"It's Juan Sebastián, and yes. That's good data however it comes to us. But I'm not authorizing it, that's not what I do."

"We know, we know." Bradly continued. "Don't worry, he's not giving permission, but he's not going to stop you from doing it either. He's on our side. He does what he does, and we do what we do."

Bradly tried some encouragement, "You do what you do, Curtis. It's what you do. You're the best at it."

Curtis was building up the confidence to make the move on his own when he felt his phone vibrate.

Don't stand too close to Bradly ;)

"I gotta go." Curtis said in a hurry. He could barely see straight knowing that Cat was nearby. Not just nearby, she could see where he was standing and who he was talking to. Thinking about that, he started to worry about the others she couldn't see if she was only looking at him.

He turned to look out for her, and back around in the other direction.

"What the fuck has got into you? Who texted you?" Bradly demanded as Curtis hustled towards the door leading outside.

No sooner than Curtis opened the door it was pulled fast from the other side. He lost his balance and found himself kneeling down and facing back inside towards Bradly, with a thin arm wielding a pistol coming in right over his shoulder.

"Stay the fuck where you are O'Sheel."

"Cat!" gasped Curtis.

"Jones." Bradly said flatly realizing Curtis had somehow kept this connection from him. "Don't hurt him, Jones. And we might find a way for you to live through this."

"If he gets hurt, it won't be my fault." Curtis couldn't handle it. This was not his type of adrenaline rush he enjoyed. He closed his eyes. "You keep your hands where I can see them. Where are the others?"

Bradly nodded towards Juan Sebastián without taking his eyes off Cat Jones. "Just me and this guy here, waiting for the captain to come up so we can talk about the haul."

"Bullshit." She fired her gun across the room shattering a window. "Where are the others?"

Bradly looked around frantically for the others. He couldn't find them directly, but the shattered glass was a great alert for them to come quickly and come bringing something to fight with. Cat counted on it and moved quickly around the room looking for what she had come for. She whispered into the ear of the frightened man she held hostage, "blueprints". Curtis opened his eyes and nodded towards the table with the blueprints.

Cat pulled on his arm encouraging him to his feet. She kept the gun aimed towards Bradly. She hadn't seen any evidence of him making a move yet, but she wasn't taking any chances. "You stay right where you are. Both of you." She hadn't forgotten about the other man, "The more people in the other room, right Curtis?". He confirmed and led her to the table. She held her aim on the Irishman and looked down at the blue prints. "Which ones?" Curtis pointed at a couple, lifted one or two up, and pointed at another.

"Well fuck Curtis, roll them up for me. Quickly now."

Curtis followed the orders and handed several prints and plans of the construction project to Cat as a door behind her opened. She tucked the rolled documents behind her next to her backpack and maneuvered back towards the door she came in. She stayed close to

Curtis now, and pulled him with her. Bradly made his way closer to Juan Sebastián, anxiously looking up and down, hoping to pull the piece tethered to his ankle. Cat's eyes darted from Bradly to the large man coming out of the other door. When she realized he had a weapon drawn already, he got most of her attention.

"Who the fuck are you?" came the demand from a woman exiting the door behind him. With two out of the room now, a third on the way, and a weapon pointed at her, Cat moved Curtis between her and them while keeping her own weapon aimed at Bradly.

"I'm sorry Curtis. This will all be over soon." She never intended on him becoming a shield for her. Not that she had planned much, but this was not on the agenda coming in.

"Why that's Cat Jones." Robert announced as he exiting the doorway aiming a second weapon in her direction. "I thought you had retired, Cat? This isn't looking good for you if you plan to go back to a peaceful setting." He saw the prints she carried and noticed she was talking more to Curtis than barking any demands at them.

"What do you want, Cat?" Robert couldn't get a good position, so he dropped the sights of his gun towards Curtis. He figured that's how Cat found them anyway. Bradly was an idiot, but not that kind of idiot. And Curtis was smitten.

No wonder he never asked questions about where she had gone, he knew! She had been telling him. More to the fact, she had been using him. Robert considered how quickly he could drop Curtis and take a shot at Cat. Or perhaps the man next to him was fixed on her. Or Bradly could take a shot. There were options, but he knew he couldn't let her leave with those blueprints.

"You want in? You want a piece?" Robert tried to coax Cat into showing herself to him.

Sandra spoke just loud enough for Robert to hear. "I don't believe that's yours to give. Jones has given us trouble all along the way. She disrupts everything and, until now, we've never been so close to catching her."

"Just let me take care of this, will you?"

Cat Jones, ever the professional, noticed the hesitation in focus. She pushed Curtis towards those that were wielding weapons, helping to block their view of her a little better.

To steady her aim, she brought her second hand up to the gun, squared up on Bradly and fired. He didn't even have time to go for his gun as he fell lifelessly to the ground. Not taking any chances, she fired one shot into the man next to him, dropping Juan Sebastián to his knees. Curtis turned back in time to see Bradly fall and the gun go off again. Cat, with quickness and precision, sheathed her gun and flung something back towards the others behind her. Curtis only knew it missed him as he turned back again.

Robert, unable to get a good view of Cat, still had Curtis lined up in his sights. After multiple gunshots, and a flash of light flying passed Curtis, he heard the thunk of a blade catching the bodyguard next to him clean in the throat. Robert turned, recognized his backup was out of commission, and pulled the trigger still aimed perfectly at Curtis Scott.

Cat Jones paused, saw Curtis fall, looked Robert up and down once, and fled.

She knew too much.

EPILOGUE

Robert Garin Carlyle sat in the front row of the plane. At first, he was excited about the extra leg room, but he found that anywhere besides the open ocean was never space enough to truly stretch his legs. He couldn't reach the magazines in front of him, and he didn't own any device that would allow him to connect to cyberspace. But he didn't feel disconnected, even though modern society would tell him he was. He felt very much tethered and very much like he knew exactly what he needed to do. The flight back to the States would give him plenty of time to plan and prepare.

He had considered finding passage over the ocean. It would have been far more comfortable for him, and, in his position now, cost was not a problem. In fact, the cost for the flight wasn't an issue either, and it saved him considerable time. Besides, he had a window seat and it was a strangely familiar view.   It wasn't the ocean, but out of his square porthole-like window the thin clouds looked like small ripples in the ocean. Just like in Liverpool when he first had the chance to watch the effects of the wind on the surface of the water, he could see where the wind had shaped these clouds. Like looking over the bow of a ship, he could focus on the waves. Only now he watched clouds peak and fall. They didn't move like the waves he was used to; these waves were stalled in time. And where he rarely was able to see deep below the ocean's waves, here he could see cities far below. The lights and roads below the clouds made him think of lost cities below the ocean. Like one of his very vivid dreams, he was lost in the thought that he was looking down upon ancient cities far below the ocean's surface. His ship had found them, and he had no way of knowing how he'd get there, but he knew his ship was in the right spot.

The flight attendant stopped by and broke his concentration.

"Two coffees, sir. Black" She said passing him two steaming cups and a couple beverage napkins.

"Yes, thank you." Robert took the cups, one in each hand. "You don't have any sugar, do you?"

"Not on me, sir, but I can grab some on the way back."

"That won't be necessary." He assured her remembering someone who would not have been able to say the same. Putting one cup down in front of the ample space before him, he removed the lid from the other and started to take a sip.

Robert grimaced at the intense heat he tried to move quickly to a safer place in his mouth. There wasn't one. Fortunately, it was a small drink and he didn't blister anything. He managed to regret that first desperate drink, swallowed quickly and reached down to remove the lid from the second cup at his feet to allow it to cool faster.

"Who drinks their coffee hot?" He said aloud as he started to blow across the top of the coffee in his hand. He was instantly lost in the ripples across the dark liquid before him. He looked outside remembering the cities out below his magical flying ship. They were gone. He was over the ocean now and the imagery wasn't quite the same. It was too familiar. He knew he was flying. He saw boats and their wakes. He did his best to see them for the first time and guess how big they were, but he knew better. He tried hard to imagine the captains were out for recreation, but this far out he knew it was all business. And likely nothing dangerous.

Perhaps these vessels actually had captains on board.

"Nothing as dangerous as this coffee." He said out loud bringing ʾttention back to the cup in front of him. He blew over the top ʾthe container as far as he could without spilling. More ʾowed him to cool it off faster. He took little sips, ʾlf to put the cup at a greater angle. He continued this game until the cup was about half full and he could put it nearly sideways to cool it off.

He began a game of equalizing the first cup, now cooled, with the other cup that was still full. The flight attendant showed up with a few packets of sugar. He thanked her, added them all to one cup and began the process of mixing from one to the other.

Balance and symmetry. It didn't matter if there was sugar or not, but if there was, it would be rationed between the entire mix. Patterns and results were ingrained so far into his mind he did not realize he was even doing it. Just as he was balancing the temperature and ingredients of these two cups of coffee, he was planning to balance the ocean's current.

Salt and heat, the weight and temperature of the water, determined where anything would go. Where everything could go. And he was lost in it's potential. From the great salty waters of the Mediterranean, to the warm waters across the equator, he was plotting the best routes and who would be the beneficiary of his strategy. They knew of the potential, but it took Robert to unlock it. He was on the right path to the top of a mountain he never knew was even there and nothing could stop him.

Nothing but her.

He would kill her.
Whatever it took, he would kill her.

Made in the USA
San Bernardino, CA
03 August 2019